OUT OF THE BLUE

Bryher is tempted into a race on her motorbike one morning, with little idea of the chain of events that will follow. A new job leads to an unexpected meeting and a whole new career. Tristan seems to think an attractive female can oil the wheels of business. Never! She might fall for another biker, or a surfer perhaps . . . but an accountant? There's certainly no future here . . . or is there?

CHRISSIE LOVEDAY

OUT OF
THE BLUE

Complete and Unabridged

LINFORD
Leicester

First published in Great Britain in 2010

First Linford Edition
published 2011

British Library CIP Data

Loveday, Chrissie.
  Out of the blue. - - (Linford romance library)
  1. Women motorcyclists- -Fiction.
  2. Accountants- -Fiction.
  3. Love stories.
  4. Large type books.
  I. Title II. Series
  823.9′2–dc22

  ISBN 978–1–4448–0690–8

Published by
F. A. Thorpe (Publishing)
Anstey, Leicestershire

Set by Words & Graphics Ltd.
Anstey, Leicestershire
Printed and bound in Great Britain by
T. J. International Ltd., Padstow, Cornwall

This book is printed on acid-free paper

1

The two powerful bikes raced side by side along the bypass. Red and blue helmets challenged each other; first blue leading, then red overtaking. The roundabout at the end was looming; one had to give way. With gritted teeth, blue twisted the accelerator and squeezed past, narrowly missing the white van as it pulled onto the roundabout. Red dropped back, cursing at being beaten. Slowing, he turned down the road that led past the estuary, wondering who his opponent had been. He smiled. Next time, he'd be on the lookout for the guy in the blue helmet with distinctive white flashing.

'I'll get you next time,' he called out, knowing nobody could hear him.

He drove his bike into the garage and began the process of returning to his normal life, the one familiar to most of his acquaintances. Leathers unzipped and hung to air, he went into the house, showered and changed into his work suit. There was nothing like a fast ride to start the day.

He wondered what Mrs Barker would make of his hobby. His devoted secretary would be shocked to think of her staid accountant boss chasing some other biker along the bypass. One of these days, he'd be caught and fined for speeding. A six o'clock start was no guarantee that the traffic police weren't around, and one of these days he would suffer.

But it was always a challenge, and worth the thrill. It kept his mind sharp and his body ready for any demands the days might bring. This morning had possibly been a mistake, he reflected. He should never have been tempted into a race. He had been weak. He drove sedately to his office in his saloon car and parked in his dedicated space. *T A Adams*, the painted sign proclaimed. Tristan Adams was ready for work.

* * *

In her rented cottage in the seaside village of St Gwillan, Bryher Jenkins finished her morning toast. *One more mug of coffee*, she allowed herself, *then I must go and pester someone else to employ me.* If she didn't get a job soon, she might have to give in and go back to living with her parents.

Every phone call was the same. 'Of course I love you both, Mum. But I have to live my own life. No, I don't want a job in Dad's company.'

'But your brother's very happy there. And all that education you have. Isn't it being wasted?'

'Education is never wasted. I just haven't decided what to do with it yet.'

'You could come home to live, and save some money. And, Bryher, what are you doing for money? You are all right, aren't you?'

'Bless you, Mum. I'm getting by just fine.'

Bryher sighed. She hadn't spoken to

either of her parents for ages. Somehow, facing this same conversation each time wore her down. What self-respecting twentysomething still lived with her parents? Nor would she ever admit to her father that she was struggling. He would immediately demand that she went to work for the family company.

All the same, her bank balance was diminishing alarmingly. If she wasn't careful, it would be more than her pride and the cottage that would have to go. Staring from the window, she cradled her favourite mug. The tide was coming in and the rocky beach looked tidy and clean, as it always did when the sea covered the pebbles. She couldn't bear to leave this glorious spot.

Her phone rang. Her friend, Bob.

'Hi, Bob. How are you?'

'Great. Fancy a surf today? I hear it's good on the south coast.'

'Job-hunting today. I've got to get some cash.'

'I can lend you some.'

'Thanks, you're a mate, but no, that's

not the idea. I need to earn.'

'So, secretary again? Or waitressing?'

'No way. And being an au pair was fine until the daddy got a bit too keen. Trouble is, I need to be here. In Cornwall. A business degree hasn't exactly opened doors for me yet.'

'I guess being named after one of the Scillies attaches you to the sea.'

'Next to biking, surfing's my greatest passion. I'm really tempted to go out with you, but surfing doesn't bring in the pennies.'

'Try biking, then. Be a courier.'

She remembered the thrill of racing early that morning and grinned.

'What a brilliant idea,' she declared. 'Maybe I'll become a motorbike courier. Gotta go. Bye, Bob — and thanks for thinking of me.'

'Who else rides the waves like you? Good luck.'

Showered and wrapped in a towel, Bryher stood in front of her wardrobe, then flung on jeans and a long-sleeved T-shirt. Perfect beneath her beloved leathers. She flicked through the phone book for local courier services. There were two in Penzance, only a few miles away. Ideal! She pulled back her long blonde hair into a ponytail and twisted it round, securing it so it would fit under her helmet. Just in case, she took a CV from the pile she'd printed and slipped it into her bike box.

Making sure she had her driving licence with her, she wriggled into her leathers, leapt onto her bike and rode sedately into the nearby town. She parked and, helmet under her arm, set off along the steep main street.

The courier office was in a quiet side street. She pushed open the door of the unimpressive glass-fronted building, jangling a fearsomely loud bell.

'Good morning,' she said brightly to the bored-looking woman behind the reception desk. 'Is the manager available?'

'If you've got a package, fill in the form on the desk. If you're here to collect, then . . . what's your name?'

The phone rang. The woman sprang to life. In a completely different voice, she announced, 'Swift Deliveries, how can I help?' She spoke into the phone, wrote down details and promised that someone would be around shortly. 'Pleased to be of service, and thank you for your call.'

Bryher stared, fascinated by the evident dual persona of the receptionist.

'So, what did you want?' the woman asked in her previous bored voice.

'A job. Is the manager available?'

'He hasn't turned up yet. Nothing new. You got a clean licence?' Bryher felt herself being scrutinised. 'Don't usually employ women for the actual deliveries but you look as if you can handle yourself. What's your name?'

'Bryher Jenkins. And yes, I have a clean licence. Been driving a bike since I was seventeen. No accidents.'

'Bit above our usual type, I must say. Doesn't pay much, but you get to keep any tips you might get. Don't have to declare them, if you get my drift. Tell you what, there's a pick-up just come in. I'll give you a chance to see what you're worth. Here.' She handed over the page she had just written and Bryher glanced at it. A package to pick up at Wyatt and Company Accountants, St Ives. Deliver to an address in Truro before noon. 'Think you can do that?'

'Sure. But don't you want my details? And what's the pay? What will your manager say if you give me a job without his say-so?'

'Don't worry about it. He'll be sweet.'

'And the money?'

'Do you want to do this run or shall I call our regular chap?'

'I'll do it,' Bryher said, anxious not to lose her chance.

'Bring the docket back with the signatures. Oh, and give me your mobile number in case anything else comes in. I'm Madge, by the way.'

As she drove along the road to St Ives, Bryher cursed her own naivety.

That woman had got away with it. Probably she would pocket the fee herself and Bryher would get nothing. Still, it was a beautiful summer morning and she was on the road on her beloved bike. She grinned, thinking how shocked her parents would be. She could hear their voices again. *Wasting your education.* Her brother Martin was altogether more conventional and had pleased their parents by enthusing about the electronics company run by their father, miles from Cornwall. Too far for her liking.

She drove round the nightmarishly narrow streets of St Ives and soon found the office; she knew the town well. A sign pointed to a customer car park at the side of the office. She took off her helmet but carried it in with her, not wanting to risk losing it.

'Good morning. Swift Deliveries. You have a package for Truro?'

Bryher handed over the sheet she had been given and the receptionist scanned it quickly. 'That's fine. I'll go and get it.

You're new, aren't you?'

'Yes. Very new. My first day.'

'They don't usually have females on their staff. Nice to see a friendly face.' The woman disappeared and came back with a bulky envelope. Bryher signed her line on the sheet and picked up the package. She nodded her thanks, pulling her helmet back on. She was just going out of the door when a voice shouted to her to stop. Turning, she saw a man approaching. He was tall, with light brown hair, and rather nice-looking.

'Sorry, is there a problem?' she asked, lifting her helmet off again. The man stared at her.

'Oh! You're — you're a woman,' he stammered in evident confusion.

Bryher nodded, smiling.

'Sorry. I thought . . . Never mind. Sorry.' He followed her to the door and looked through the window at the bike parked outside. 'Striking helmet. Did you customise it yourself?'

'Well, yes, my design. Why?' What

interest was it to this bloke in a suit?

'I er, well, I thought I saw one like it before. Unusual.'

'It represents waves and seabirds. A sort of geometric depiction. I love the sea, and I'm as passionate about surfing as I am about my bike.'

'Wow! Interesting. Well, I mustn't keep you, or I'll be complaining you didn't meet the deadline. No doubt we'll meet again, er — ?'

'Bryher. Bye, then.'

Good-looking chap, she mused, as she climbed on her bike. *And what on earth was all that about my helmet?* She sped along the A30 towards Truro, taking care to avoid setting off the speed cameras. Time was pressing if she was to make it by midday. She wondered why people didn't get papers organised to go by mail. The cost of a courier service must far exceed the post — but why should she care? She might have a fairly permanent job if she performed well. It would do for the time being, anyway.

Bryher hurried into the office in the middle of the busy town of Truro without removing her helmet. The receptionist immediately picked up the phone and told her to take off the helmet before she called security.

Bryher put down the large packet and lifted off the helmet.

'Sorry. I wasn't thinking.'

'We don't allow anyone in here unless we can see them properly. Too many thieves could use it as a disguise.' The receptionist was a pretty young woman, immaculately dressed and with long polished nails that left Bryher wondering how she could possibly type without breaking them. 'Do you have the form for me to sign?'

'Yes — of course.' Bryher took the paper from her pocket and handed it over. The girl stamped it and made a squiggle to represent a name. 'Thanks,' Bryher said, staring at it. 'Sorry, can't read your name. What do you do here?'

'Financial services. Insurance, that sort of thing.'

'Oh. So why do you have to use an accountant?'

'I beg your pardon?'

'The package. It came from an accountant. If you're in financial services, why do you need an accountant? And if so, why not use one a bit closer? There must be dozens of them in Truro.'

'Excuse me. What's it to you?' the girl asked snappily.

'Just showing an interest. I didn't mean anything. I'll be on my way.'

'Audit. Have to have an independent audit. Actually, hang on a minute. I'll get a signature from the boss and you can take it back to Mr Adams.'

'Okay. Is this normal? Only this is my first day and I wasn't told I should have to return to St Ives.'

'Is it a problem?'

'Course not. I was just wondering about the fees.'

The girl looked pityingly at the

leather-clad figure in front of her.

'You certainly are new to this game, aren't you? I'll get the signature.'

It was almost one o'clock when Bryher arrived back in St Ives. Mr Adams was coming out of the door as she was taking off her helmet once more and Bryher smiled at him in recognition.

'I've got your receipt from the Truro place. Think I'm supposed to get yet another signature from you. Is this normal? All this to and fro-ing?'

'I guess so. At least you get to ride your bike for nothing. You must enjoy it or you wouldn't be doing the job. Nothing like the rush of speed, is there?'

Bryher nodded slowly, staring at the vision before her. He was wearing a dark suit, spotless white shirt, immaculate silk tie and polished leather shoes. What on earth did he know about the rush of speed? He was an accountant! The epitome of boring convention. Still good-looking, though. Must be about thirty, and devastating eyes. Like liquid chocolate.

'I'm just going for a bite to eat. Want to join me?'

'I . . . I'm not sure.' The invitation caught her by surprise.

'Do you have to get back?'

'I don't really know. But I'm hardly dressed for lunch anywhere. Besides, why would you ask a mere bike courier?'

'You're obviously a bright lady. You sound as if you had an education.'

'I really don't know what you mean by that. I've barely spoken to you.'

'And you interest me. Besides being rather lovely.'

Bryher felt irritated by what she saw as a rather patronising attitude.

'I think not, thank you. Lunch, I mean.'

'I'm sorry. I've offended you. I was trying to compliment you. My name's Tristan, by the way. Yours?'

'Bryher. I told you that earlier.' A flicker of annoyance crossed his face but he smiled.

'After the island? Unusual. Please, come and share a pasty with me. Or have a whole one, if you like. The shop just along here makes the best pasties in Cornwall. We can sit and watch the sea while we eat.'

He gave her a dazzling smile that brooked no more argument. Besides, she realised she was extremely hungry.

They sat side by side on the sea wall and watched as a few surfers tried to catch a ride on the poor waves.

'Not much surf today,' Bryher remarked.

'Where do you usually go?'

'I live in St Gwillan so when the tide's right, that's as good as anywhere.'

'And where do you like to ride your bike?'

'Anywhere. Everywhere.'

'Speed limits are a bit of a handicap, aren't they?'

'Mmm. Just occasionally I . . . well, I admit to going a bit fast.'

'Along the bypass, for instance?'

Bryher stared. 'How . . . ? You ride yourself, do you?' She hoped he wasn't

16

some sort of traffic cop in his spare time.

He gave a wicked grin and shrugged his shoulders. 'Must get back to work. Thanks for your company. Maybe see you on the bypass sometime?'

She stared at him again. What was this about the bypass? She remembered Red Helmet that morning. Never. It couldn't be him. She gave him a questioning smile. His face remained impassive.

'I'll doubtless see you again. Good for Tony Swift, taking on an attractive courier for once. Much better than his usual spotty youths.' He strode into the office with a hand raised in farewell.

'Thanks for the pasty,' she called after him.

★ ★ ★

'You were gone a long time,' Madge said accusingly when Bryher finally arrived back at the office.

'They wanted me to take a signature

back to St Ives. I grabbed a bite to eat afterwards. Here you are, a collection of papers and signatures.'

'That's good. Double run, in effect. Tony — Mr Swift — will like that. Give me your address and that, and we'll be in touch. Pay at the end of the month. You want more work if it comes in?'

'Yes, of course. How often is it likely to be? I need a regular income.'

'Should be good. I'll call tomorrow. On your mobile?'

'Fine. Thanks.' Madge was certainly brief with her words.

Back at home, Bryher reflected on her odd day. Tristan's face kept floating into her mind. She wondered about his comments regarding bikes and speed and for just a moment, wondered if he really could have been the speeding biker she had challenged and beaten that morning.

An accountant? Never. Besides, the chance of meeting him later that day was far too great a coincidence to believe.

All the same, six o'clock tomorrow morning would find her on the bypass again. Only tomorrow, she would not be racing. Too risky, now she was dependent on her bike to earn money.

2

At six-fifteen the next day Tristan rode along the bypass for the second time. No sign of the biker with the blue helmet and blue leathers. He went around the roundabout one more time, and rode back slightly more sedately. Going in the other direction, he spotted her. The dual carriageway prevented him from catching her and he gave up, going back to his house with a feeling of failure. Perhaps it wasn't even the same girl.

He smiled, a plan forming in his mind. He didn't even know why she'd made such an impact on him. A bike courier? He was certain there was more to her than that. He'd find an excuse to call Swift Deliveries again and ask for her by name. Besides, if she turned out to be reliable and discreet, there were plenty of opportunities he could find to employ her. Someone who didn't mind taking a few risks could be very useful.

He needed to know more about her and her background. A good excuse to ask her out. Maybe he should take up surfing. He rode back home and began the transformation into his daytime self.

Bryher smiled as she saw Red Helmet going along the other lane. He was certainly travelling at speed and she was secretly glad she didn't need to compete. Maybe she should give up her morning trips, just in case she was spotted. Certainly speeding with another bike giving chase was going to be more noticeable. She accelerated a little, worried that she might be getting a little too conscientious. She was right at the top edge of the speed limit.

Her mobile rang just as she was safely home and finishing her second cup of coffee. 'You good for a job?' Madge asked without preamble. 'Made a hit yesterday. Adams wants you again, to deliver to Redruth this time.'

'That's great. Do I come to the office

first? It's the opposite direction.'

'You'll have to, or you won't have the forms to get signatures and then payment. Note all mileage for expenses. Soon as.' She hung up.

Chatty lady, thought Bryher dryly. She showered and dressed in record time and was soon on her way to Penzance to collect the paperwork and then to St Ives. The Wyatt and Company car park was full and she stopped behind the car owned by T A Adams, according to the sign. Presumably, Tristan would not need to get his car out in the next few minutes.

Carrying her helmet again, she went into the reception area.

'You again,' the receptionist remarked. 'How can I help?'

'Package to go to Redruth?'

'Sorry. I don't know anything about it. Any idea who placed the order?' Long red fingernails tapped on a few keys.

'Mr Adams? I think that's what I was told.'

'One moment, please. I'll call him.'

Bryher looked around the plush waiting area. No wonder accountants charged so much money. Posh offices, and sending everything by courier. Not that she was complaining. She was earning money, and hoped she wouldn't need to employ an accountant any time soon.

She turned, hearing a door open, and smiled as Tristan approached her.

'Oh, good,' he said with a grin. 'I was hoping they'd send you.'

'I was told you'd requested me. Thanks. Not sure why, though.'

'I wanted to see you again. Need your advice.'

'My advice? Heavens. I can't think why.'

'I'm thinking of taking up surfing. I thought you might help me choose a board and whatever else I need. How about dinner with me tonight? You can give me all the advice I need.' He smiled a rather devastating smile.

'Why me?' she demanded.

'You're knowledgeable about such things. And I'd like to know more about you. You don't seem like the normal couriers we usually have here.'

Aware of the startled looks she was getting from Long Nails, she turned and looked squarely into the man's lovely eyes. How could she say no?

'Okay. But I'm not sure you really need my help. Any half-decent surf shop will advise you.'

'Give me your address. I'll pick you up at seven-thirty if that's all right. Just casual. I thought we might go to a lovely little pub I know. Great food and live music on Thursdays.'

'Shame it's only Wednesday, then, isn't it?' she replied with a giggle.

'We'll just have to go again tomorrow then, won't we?' he countered.

'You have a delivery for me to take to Redruth?'

'Oh, yes, of course. Take it to the flower shop, top of the High Street. Deliver it directly to Carole. Your address? For this evening.' He gave her a sheet of paper and she scribbled it down for him.

'Can you sign my docket, please? Or I won't get paid.'

He gave her a wry grin. 'Costing me a fortune, all this. I'll look forward to seeing you later. Thanks.'

Bryher said goodbye to Long Nails and went out with the rather small envelope tucked into her pocket. It occurred to her that this was an entirely contrived errand, but so what? It was a job. Tristan was hardly someone she'd mind seeing again. And again.

★ ★ ★

The florist's in Redruth was easy to find. Bryher was able to stop at the kerbside. She unhooked her helmet and went in. A slightly familiar-looking woman with long hair and lovely brown eyes was behind the counter.

'Good morning,' Bryher began. 'I have a letter for you from Wyatt and Company, St Ives.' Where might she have seen the woman before?

'Oh, yes. Tristan phoned to say that you were on your way. Thanks.' She gave a knowing grin as she took the envelope from her. 'Trust my brother.'

'Your brother?' That explained it. There was a distinct resemblance.

'Yes. He always finds complicated ways to do everything. I'm Carole, by the way. And you must be Bryher. Love the name.'

'Thanks. I did wonder about this delivery — the receptionist seemed to know nothing about it. He's just made it up, hasn't he?'

Carole raised her eyebrows. 'He wanted to see you. That's all.'

Bryher blushed. 'Not that I'd expect you to say anything else, but there's nothing I should know, is there? About him, I mean.'

'Not at all. He's a lovely bloke. Bit mad at times, but very good-hearted. Set me up in this shop. My dream job. I assume he's asked you out?'

'Dinner, this evening. Hope I did the right thing in agreeing. Can you sign my delivery note, please? Or I won't get paid. Though I do feel a bit guilty.'

'Don't be. He can afford it. Enjoy your evening.'

Bryher rode back to Penzance, her mind occupied by the strange morning. She could scarcely believe anyone like Tristan had to go to such lengths to get a date. He was gorgeous, and evidently well-off. Why should he pick her? She was relatively ordinary-looking and if you took away her slight addiction to motorbikes and surfing, not even very interesting.

There were a couple more deliveries that day and she began to think there might be something to her job after all. She also met the company owner, Tony Swift.

'Madge told me you were keen for work. Need someone reliable. Few rules we need you to know about. Keep your mileage details for when you put in your claims. Keep your licence clean, and make sure you're available when we need you. You should do well. Nice-looking lady like you. Our male clients will like that.'

Bryher glared. This attitude infuriated her, but she held her breath and managed not to respond. She needed the job, for now at least.

'Do you need me again today?'

'No. You can get off home now. We'll call when we need you. Nice to have you on board,' Tony told her.

★ ★ ★

Back home, she was relaxing with some tea when there was a knock at the door. 'Flowers for Miss Bryher,' the cheerful van driver announced. He handed her a pretty basket of delicate flowers.

'How lovely — but there's a mistake. It isn't my birthday or anything.'

'Well, here they are. Clear as you can want. Carole's Flowers, Redruth.' Light dawned. She knew exactly who had sent them.

'Ah. Thank you. Nobody sends me flowers, so I was surprised.'

'Enjoy. Somebody obviously cares.' He walked down the path whistling.

Bryher scarcely needed to look at the card. She must have taken the order herself, in the special courier-delivered envelope. What a strange thing to have done. *Why on earth is Tristan making such a big thing of all this?* she wondered for the umpteenth time. *Surely he must have some sort of motive other than just a dinner date?*

Still perplexed, she went upstairs to shower and change. Good job he'd said to be casual; her wardrobe did not extend to anything else. Her more formal clothes were still stored at her parents' house, that being the only place she was likely to need them. Her lifestyle was not part of the County set any more. 'Been there, done that,' she so often said when her parents invited her to some boring function. *You really ought to go and see them soon, though,* her conscience told her.

She put on her best jeans and a fairly new T-shirt.

Right on time, Tristan knocked on the door.

'Lovely cottage,' he said, just as she was thanking him for the flowers.

'Do you want to come in, or shall we head straight off?'

'Let's go. Gets busy later, and I'm starving. You look nice.'

'Thanks. I wasn't sure how casual 'casual' was. You don't look bad yourself.' He was wearing fawn chinos and a corduroy shirt that matched his eyes. Quite a contrast to the dark grey suit she had seen before.

* * *

The food was home-cooked and simple, but very tasty. They both drank beer, a local brew that Bryher was fond of.

'I always feel I should ask for something more sophisticated,' she confessed, 'but I love a beer occasionally.'

'Me too — and this place keeps a very good pint. You want another?'

'I won't, thanks. Now I have to earn my living on the road, I daren't risk losing my licence — or even getting points on it.'

'I gather you haven't been doing

30

courier work for long?'

'Two days now. I'm quite enjoying myself, although they've been a bit coy about telling me what my wages will be. They said I get to keep tips, but I haven't had any so far. Sorry — that wasn't meant to be a hint. I suppose the flowers were a tip, really. Did I actually deliver the order myself?'

'How did you guess? I had to phone with the address later, though.'

'Bit devious, wasn't it? Suppose it wasn't me who came for the job?'

'I'd asked for you. They know not to disappoint me. I'm a very good client. Look, I have a proposition for you. No, don't look like that! A job.'

'A job? You hardly know me. You don't know anything about my background. Anyhow, I thought you wanted to talk to me about surfing.'

'Later. I'd like you to come and work for me. Still some sort of courier work, but on a much larger scale. Abroad, even. What do you think?'

'Sounds wonderful, but I'd need to

know a whole lot more before I could even consider it. You've quite knocked me off my perch.'

'Do you speak any languages?'

'Well, yes, as a matter of fact. My degree is in business studies and I did French and Spanish as subsidiary subjects.'

He beamed. 'I knew I was on to something with you.'

'But why does a Cornish accountant need a courier who can speak foreign languages?'

'Only occasionally working abroad. Mostly around here — but I have ambitions. Besides, I have fingers in more pies than Wyatt and Company.'

'Really?' Bryher was intrigued.

'I only work part time in St Ives. The rest of my time is spent in a more — how shall I say it? — a more *practical* environment. My role in the practice is really temporary until my business takes off properly. Helps pay the bills. I think I'd go mad if I was doing company audits all the time.'

'So, what's this business you're hoping may take off?'

'Oh, this and that. Bit of a mixture really. Some acquisitions. Some security work.'

'Exactly what does that mean?'

'Simplistically, I suppose it's better known as property development.'

'I see.' Bryher leaned back in her chair.

'Are you interested?'

'Well, yes. I'd be interested to know a bit more. I only see my present job as a very temporary thing. To restore my bank balance a little.'

They talked for a long time after their meal, drinking coffee and discovering more about each other. Bryher realised she was doing most of the talking, and had learned only a little of Tristan's real life. She knew he had a sister, and was unmarried. He lived alone in his own home, not far from hers. He worked two or three days a week for the accountant and mostly from home on the other days. He was very easy to talk to and had the knack of extracting information without giving much away. On the other hand, she felt that this was almost a job interview rather than just a social occasion and didn't mind that she had told him so much.

'More coffee?' she offered as they arrived back at her cottage.

'I shall be kept awake if I drink any more coffee. So, thanks, but no.' He touched her arm shyly as they stood beside the car. 'Think about my offer. We'll meet tomorrow. I'm sure you must have many more questions.'

'I'll make a list. The only downside that I can see is that I don't want to be away from Cornwall for long. I get unsettled when I can't see the sea for a few days. But if it's a case of short trips, then it sounds fine. I need time to think, and then loads of answers. Thanks for a most interesting evening.'

'I'll see you on the by-pass tomorrow morning. Early. Winner takes all?' With a wicked grin, he got back into his car and drove away.

Bryher closed her door, her heart pounding. He was Red Helmet. She was sure of it. He'd as much as admitted it. She'd beaten him once; she could do it again. Trouble was, she had to stick to the speed limit now. What did he have in mind with his 'winner takes all' comment? Something other than racing motorbikes . . .

*　★　★

Bryher spent a restless night, tossing and turning. When she did fall asleep she dreamed she was chasing down the bypass, dropping flowers everywhere. When she awoke, it was almost eight o'clock and much too late for an early ride. She still felt dubious about Tristan's offer of work but it was the best offer she had ever had, apart from her father's company.

There were no calls from Swift's the following day. She stayed around the house in case anyone phoned and she was needed in a hurry. She made a list of questions to ask Tristan. Carefully, she put salary low down her list in case he thought she was merely mercenary.

Among her thoughts of a possible job, Tristan himself loomed large. She kept going back to the thought, *why her?* He'd made his offer before he knew anything at all about her. She was certainly attracted to him and flattered by the attention of such a successful man, but she felt concerned that he was making this job offer without thinking it through and it could all fade to nothing.

On the other hand, she hadn't got anything else in the pipeline and she wasn't making any huge commitment.

By the time evening came, her mobile phone had been strangely quiet for the entire day. She had heard nothing from Tristan, and began to think about an evening meal. After all, he'd only said they would talk again; nothing specific about eating together. She looked in her small freezer and took out a ready-made fish pie. Boring, but adequate.

She put it into the microwave and poured herself a glass of wine.

Then she heard a car stop outside and looked through the window. It was him. Tristan. Why hadn't he called? She put the wine in the fridge and turned off the microwave, waiting for him to knock.

'Hi. Sorry I couldn't call you. I didn't take your number. Are you ready for a night of music and food?'

'I wasn't sure you'd remembered. I'd offer you something to eat if I had something worth offering. There's a glass of wine, though.'

'I won't, thanks — not now. I promised you music and there's always food available, as you know.'

'Okay, thanks — I'll just get my list of questions.'

'Good — that must mean you're considering my offer.'

'Maybe. I need to know lots more, though. About you — and your offer.'

'Let's go, then.'

3

At the same pub as the previous evening, they chose meals from the extensive menu and settled into a relatively quiet corner.

'The band starts at eight, so we need to talk first. Once it gets going, you can't hear yourself think.'

'I don't know why I've never found this place before. It's great. We usually go to the beach bar after surfing. So, who's playing tonight?'

'Local group. They're getting known around here. A mixture of folk and rock. Okay, you've got your list? Actually, *I* have a couple of questions.'

'Fine. Ask away.'

'I take it you are unattached? No dependents or anything?'

'Nobody special. Loads of friends. Well — a few friends, lots of surfer and biker mates. Why do you ask?'

'I just don't want to get beaten up in

a dark alley by some jealous man.'

'And I don't want to be sued by a jealous wife. There really isn't one?'

'Never had time to look for the right person. I told you I was single last night, didn't I?'

'Just checking. Consistent. Good answer.' Bryher gave her quirky smile.

'Fire away, then. What do you want to know?'

'Well, what makes you think I can do the job, whatever it is?'

'You're feisty. You like speed, so I assume you don't like hanging around. Just what I need.'

'You know this how?'

He smiled. 'Well, I'll confess to having a bike and a red helmet.'

'I knew it had to be you,' she exclaimed. 'Coincidences are often too hard to believe. That we should meet so soon after our — well, I suppose you might call it a race.' She paused and looked more thoughtful. 'But I still don't know why you think I can do whatever it is you need me to do.'

'Gut instinct. Go on.'

'Okay. What exactly is the job?'

'I buy speculative building sites and properties to repair and turn around for a profit. I need to act quickly at times and can't always be there to close a deal. Can't always be at auctions — or maybe it's just the need to get in before the competition from others, you know the sort of thing. Once a deal is done, papers need couriering around. I spend a small fortune on dealing with the companies, so having someone of my own would make sense. How am I doing so far?'

Their meals arrived and the band began to play, so the conversation came to a halt. 'This chilli's fantastic,' she shouted between mouthfuls.

'Usually is. My pie's equally good. What do you think of the music?'

'Excellent.' The next number began so any further chat was impossible.

At the end Tristan said with a grin, 'You haven't asked about money.'

'Didn't want to appear totally mercenary. What are you offering?'

He named a modest figure, but it was much more than she had earned before, so she nodded. 'Okay, but I'm assuming this is for starters?'

'It's what I can manage at the moment. As things grow and if it works out between us, yes, it's for starters.'

She learned a little more about the demands she would be facing and so far, nothing was putting her off. 'Do you want my CV?' she asked.

'If you like. But I'd guess it wouldn't help me much. If you've got a degree, that says something about you. But the reason you're not using it interests me more.'

'Any offers I had meant moving away from Cornwall. I've been living off savings, earning enough to keep me surfing and biking. When do I start?'

'Next week suit you? Do you have to give notice to Tony Swift?'

'I doubt it. I haven't signed anything. Just did a few runs for him, but nothing more. Don't suppose he'll be too delighted. I gather he has a few problems keeping his staff.'

'He pays peanuts, though he charges his clients well enough. He's a lazy blighter but Madge keeps things going. Plenty of lads like the idea of biking round the countryside but they don't stay long.'

'Right then, I'll resign tomorrow and collect my wages so far.'

At the end of the evening, they drove back to her cottage. Tristan gave her a peck on the cheek and took her hand.

'This is going to work out, I'm sure of it. I'm glad I found you. Oh, I forgot — you never did give me the advice I need about surfing.'

'You never gave me the chance. I thought that was just a line you were shooting. If you're serious, why not come over on Saturday if you've got time? I'll give you a lesson. You can hire the gear at the shop by the beach. If you like it well enough, we'll discuss whether you need buy anything.'

'Give me your phone number.'

'Give me yours. I can call you and you'll have mine recorded on yours.' He typed in his number on her mobile and she rang it. 'There you go. More efficient,' she said. 'See you Saturday morning. Tide's coming in at seven, so soon after eight is good.'

'You know these sort of things? Amazing. Obviously an early riser.'

'It pays off. Gets you jobs, new friends and the occasional basket of flowers. Quite a week.'

'And you're quite a girl, aren't you?'

She gave him a wave and ran up her path. She was slightly pleased that he didn't see her delighted grin. It might have taken something away from her apparently feisty image.

She glanced at her watch. Eleven o'clock. She was bursting to tell someone about her good fortunes. She dialled her friend Bob's number.

'Bryher. What's up? Broken down somewhere? I can't come out to you. Had a bit too much to drink but I can probably organise something.'

'You're a pal but no, it's nothing like that. Guess what? I've got a job.'

'Doing what?'

'It's all a bit complicated. Some courier work. Helping someone buy and sell stuff. Quite a high-powered chap actually. He even sent me flowers.'

'Good heavens. Not one of us, then?'

'Not at all. Though he does have a bike and he wants to learn to surf.'

'Can't be all bad. Take care of yourself though, hon. If he doesn't treat you right, let us know and we'll be round to sort him out.'

'Crazy guy. I can hear noises. Who's with you?'

'Three — or is it four? — of the lads. Come and join us at my place.'

'Thanks but I need my beauty sleep. Just wanted to tell you my news.'

'Good on ya. Drinks are on you on Saturday night.'

'Maybe. Goodnight. Love you all, you idiots!' She hugged herself and danced around her tiny living room. Life was suddenly good. And having the gorgeous, chocolate-eyed Tristan for a boss! That was quite something.

* ★ ★

Just for fun, Bryher took an early drive along the bypass. She stuck to the speed limit, frowning at herself for suddenly showing such a responsible attitude. Somehow, she felt as if she'd grown up in the last couple of days and didn't want to break laws any more. If Tristan wanted to race, he'd have to find someone else to challenge. She turned off the road and went home. Her first task was to go to the Swift office, claim her payment and give herself the sack. After a quick breakfast and shower, she set off for Penzance.

The office seemed gloomier than ever and Madge even more short-tempered than usual.

'Oh, it's you. We've got nothing for you. In fact, we might have been a bit premature in taking you on. Sorry, but that's how it is in this business. You've got a bit of pay to come, but one of the regular lads got a bit stroppy when he heard we'd taken you on.'

'That's all right. I'm not sure the job would have kept me going long. If you pay me what I'm owed, I'll be on my way.'

Bryher smiled to herself. That was very convenient. She didn't have to admit that she'd been virtually poached by one of their major clients.

Madge fingered through various sheets in her files, pulled out a few and tapped figures into a calculator. 'Not much, I'm afraid, but with the credit crunch and that, our overheads swallow up a lot of the cash. I'll put a cheque in the post. Have to get Tony to sign it.'

'I see. So how much is it?'

When she was told, she gasped. 'That barely pays the petrol. My time must be worth less than a pound an hour, in that case.'

'Oh, I forgot the mileage. There's an extra few quid on top of that.'

'Thanks anyway. I certainly can't afford to work for your organisation so it's just as well you don't want me. I'll look forward to receiving my cheque.

Nice to meet you,' she added cynically.

'Yeah, whatever,' Madge replied, her mind on her magazine beneath the counter. As she left, Bryher wondered if she would ever see her cheque.

* * *

Saturday was bright and sunny with a light wind. Bryher looked out at the surf. It was very slight and held little prospect for an exciting morning. It might be reasonable for Tristan's first outing, but not much of a challenge.

It was six-thirty. Plenty of time for breakfast before he arrived. She made toast and coffee and sat in the window seat she loved so much, overlooking the glorious bay. Just after seven o'clock, a biker with a familiar red helmet pulled up outside. The tall figure strode up the path and she opened the door before he knocked.

'Morning. You're prompt. Do you want coffee? Toast?' she offered.

'Coffee would be good, but I'm

afraid I don't really eat breakfast.'

'I'll make you some toast. I'm not having you out in the waves all morning with nothing inside you.'

'Are you always this bossy? I might have to think again about employing you. I thought we had to be in the water by eight?'

'The surf shop doesn't open till half past, so there's plenty of time. Don't you want to take your jacket off? What have you got underneath? For under the wet suit, I mean.' She blushed, realising what she was saying.

'Now there's something I'm not usually asked at this time of day. Under the leathers I have swimming shorts and a T-shirt. I also have spares on the bike to change afterwards. Hope that meets with your approval.'

'Sounds fine.' She busied herself pouring coffee to cover her confusion.

She was unused to her heart beating this fast and tried to take deep breaths inconspicuously to recover herself. 'Right. Milk? Sugar?'

'Black, please. And thanks for looking after me. You're right, I should eat breakfast. We shall begin our working days with breakfast. I'll get a coffee machine and toaster to keep in the office.'

'Sounds very civilised. Where's the office, by the way?'

'In my garden. It's a converted summer house, if I'm honest. Quite large, though, and warm. How are your computer skills?'

'Nothing too clever or complicated but I can do most basic stuff. I've got a laptop so I'm not too out of touch.'

After breakfast, they prepared for the morning's surfing. Bryher quicky changed into her wet suit and picked up her board and bag of necessities.

'You're very organised. I like that,' Tristan told her. 'Okay to leave my stuff here?'

They walked down to the beach and the surf shop where he collected everything he needed. The wet suit looked good on his lean figure and Bryher watched him walking down the slope, realising she felt proud to be with him. He gave her a grin.

'Must say, wet suits don't leave a lot to the imagination, despite almost a hundred percent coverage. You look very good.' She blushed as his eyes roamed over her.

'Thanks. I was thinking the same thing. So, have you done any surfing?'

'Just a bit. Holidays when I was a kid. Never got further than kneeling.'

'It's a start. Okay, let's surf.'

With the slight surf, they did little more than use the waves to ride in, lying flat on the boards. Bryher felt her pupil was going to prove a good surfer. He was strong and athletic and able to move quickly and nimbly. But she was frustrated at the lack of excitement with the tiny waves. At almost midday she'd had enough.

'Shall we call it a day?' she shouted to Tristan.

'If you like,' he replied. 'Not much going on, is there?'

They paddled into the shore and

walked up the beach, the heavy boards under their arms.

'What did you think?' she asked.

'Think I could take to it. I'd like to give it another go with a bit more height to the waves.' He peeled off his wet suit back at the shop and handed it back. The assistant took it to the side of the shop where it was hosed down and hung to dry. Bryher looked admiringly at his surprisingly muscular body as he stood in his swimming shorts and wet T-shirt. His hair was still wet and looked much darker. He smiled at her.

'Actually, I'd be really grateful if I could have a shower and get changed before I go back home. Would that be all right?'

'Of course. Let's go.'

An hour later, showered and changed, they were drinking hot chocolate, sitting out in the tiny garden.

'So, what are you doing with the rest of your weekend?' Tristan asked.

'Suppose I'd better do some shopping. Washing. Cleaning. All the usual exciting stuff. So I'm ready to devote myself to my job on Monday.'

He laughed. 'Sounds riveting. I'm planning a scouting trip tomorrow.'

'What, camping in woods? Rubbing sticks together?'

'Idiot. No, I'm going to drive around and make notes of possible projects. You might like to tag along? I can promise you a decent lunch at some point. If you're interested, of course.'

'It's really a day's work, in fact?' she teased.

'I s'pose. But I don't offer a decent Sunday lunch on working days. Thought you might like a change from washing and whatever else was on your list. Could cut down on your shopping time if I buy lunch.'

'Okay. Sounds interesting and maybe it'll give me some insight into how you work. Do you want a toasted sandwich or something now? Don't know about you, but I'm starving. That's the best I can offer.'

'Great. Then I must head off. I've got

an agenda myself — cleaning, shopping, washing. You know the sort of thing we bachelors have to do.'

Not wanting to lose touch with her old friends, Bryher went along to their usual beach bar haunt that evening. It was good to be with the lads but she couldn't help feeling they were sometimes a bit too full-on with their chat about surf and bikes. There were few other topics of conversation, and she had the dreaded feeling that she was growing away from them a little.

'So who was the guy you were surfing with this morning?' asked Bob.

'My new boss. He wants to learn to surf, so I thought I'd help him.'

'Not a bad start. He's done it before, though, hasn't he?'

'As a kid on holiday, or so he said.'

'Hmm. Something about the way he handled himself. I reckon he's a bit more than a beginner.'

'You think so? Why should he tell me he wants to learn?'

'He fancies you. Wants you to help

him, and it makes you feel good.'

'Nah. Rubbish. He doesn't fancy me at all. Why would he?'

'Gather round, lads. She's fishing for compliments. What do we see in her?' Bob led the group in teasing her. She giggled as the banter went on.

'Okay, I give in. I'll buy the next round. Anyway, why aren't you all spending your Saturday evening with gorgeous girls instead of hunkering down in the bar with your mates?'

'Just because it's Saturday. It's what we do on Saturdays. And though you're female, you're here because you're an honorary mate.'

'You're mad, you lot. I'm sure I'm over the moon to be an honorary mate. But I'm starting a whole new adventure tomorrow.' She sighed. 'I'm sorry, but I think I'm about to grow up. I thought I'd done that when I went away to uni but it was all too easy to fall back into old habits.'

'Does this mean your days of racing along the bypass are over?'

'Maybe. But some habits are too old to give up completely.'

'You'll get caught one of these days.'

'Maybe I already did. Cheers, lads. Wish me luck. I think I might need it.'

4

Tristan in working mode was a whole new person. He stopped outside the cottage soon after eight the next morning. Bryher was still finishing her coffee and invited him in for a cup. He was impatient to get on the road but waited for her to finish, handing her a map and clipboard and talking nonstop. He was clearly excited by his plans for the day.

'Right, here's the deal. We'll drive along the south coast starting in the far west, looking for any properties — derelict or otherwise — for sale. Your job is to make notes on what we see and describe the exact location. If any of them have sales boards outside, note down the agent and a phone number.'

'And what will you be doing while I'm so busy?'

'Driving on to the next place.

Actually, we'll collect my camera and take pictures too.'

'Or use a video camera, and you can make a commentary as we go.'

'Brilliant idea. Though I'll still want a written record of exactly where the places are. Saves time identifying it later.'

Bryher was fascinated by his ability to make quick judgments on what could be satisfactory and what was useless. Sometimes he would look at a wreck of a barn and want extra notes taking. She felt embarrassed stopping and looking inside some places, feeling it was intruding on private property.

'Nonsense. If they want to sell, I might be the very one — the only one — keen to buy it. Come on. Where's that feisty girl who came to work for me?'

'You must have a fortune if you're considering spending so much.'

'Well, yes, I have money at my disposal, but it's not all mine. I have a business partner. He's largely a sleeping partner but we meet regularly to discuss progress and strategies. Okay. There's a barn down the next turning. I saw it on the Internet and it looks promising. Camera ready? Stills first, then we'll do some video as we look around it.'

They drove down a narrow lane with grass growing along the middle. Bryher looked anxious as his car bumped over loose stones, hoping the lane didn't end over a steep cliff drop.

'What's up?' Tristan asked, noticing her expression.

'I can't see any sign of a barn and we're heading straight for the sea. I was just hoping the road doesn't end too suddenly.'

'You're not as brave as you like me to think, are you?' He grinned.

'I'm not on my bike and driving myself.'

'Fair enough. And, you're right. Even if there is a barn down here, it's not a suitable site for a team of builders to develop. Imagine getting concrete delivered down here. I'll turn in the next gap and we'll try somewhere else.'

'Let's hope there is a 'next gap'.'

Soon after midday, they stopped to look at the map. There were several small villages near the coast, so they decided to drive on before looking for somewhere to stop and eat. It was amazing how many little lanes there were, ending in tiny hamlets or single dwellings.

'You know, I never realised there are so many little places tucked away. It must be very daunting living so far away from everywhere, especially when the winter gales are blowing,' Bryher commented. 'Once you're down some of these lanes, it's difficult to find a place to turn.'

'That's quite a consideration. Development costs will be high where access is difficult and little space to park. Besides, who will want some high-cost new home if they can't reach it some of the time? I think we might skip some of the narrowest places.'

Bryher felt pleased that he'd accepted

her comment as being useful.

They drove into a popular holiday village, one Bryher knew well from her surfing. The road was lined with houses that could have been built in any town in Britain. Tristan glanced at the various For Sale signs, but didn't slow down. He turned in the car park and drove away again.

'What's down there?' He indicated a stony track running beside the sea.

'A few houses. The road rejoins the main road further on.'

He turned down the track and they bounced along over potholes. 'Still not good for builders' vehicles. You sure we can get out at the other end?'

'Certain,' she confirmed. 'We come here surfing occasionally.'

They reached a layby. The No Parking signs looked hostile, but Tristan stopped anyway. He got out to look at the magnificent bay.

'What a spot. Wait a minute. Look at that cottage. Looks empty.' He pushed open the gate and went down the path through a lovely garden. Feeling she might be intruding, Bryher followed him, hoping there wasn't anyone living there, watching through the closed curtains. She needed to get over this feeling if she was to be successful in this new job. Tristan was peering in through gaps in the curtains and tapping at the exterior walls.

'Empty, as I thought. Gorgeous little place. I love it. Take some pictures, will you? Roof looks poor. Been empty a while. I'm going round the back.'

Bryher gave a shrug. *Get over it*, she told herself and she took out the camera. This is what she'd signed up for — except she hadn't actually signed anything yet. The whole place seemed deserted.

'This looks ideal,' Tristan announced as he returned. 'Poor condition. Perfect spot and probably for sale at a good price.' They went back up the path and saw a woman walking her dog. She stopped to watch the pair.

'Can I help?' she said aggressively.

'My wife and I are interested in this cottage,' Tristan announced. Bryher raised her eyebrows. *Wife?* 'Can you tell us anything? Is it for sale?'

'I believe there's an agent. You'd have to contact them. They don't like people wandering around the garden, willy-nilly.'

'It's just the sort of thing we're looking for, isn't it, darling?' Tristan said with a smile, putting his arm round her shoulder. Bryher rather liked the feeling and smiled back, though she was annoyed at his presumption.

'Perfect, dearest,' she replied. She noticed him biting the corner of his mouth as he stifled a grin.

'Do you know which agent it's with?'

'You'd need to look it up on this www thing everyone talks about. Now please shut the gate and move your car from the No Parking area.'

'Thank you very much for your help,' Tristan said, his most winning smile on his handsome face. Bryher noticed the elderly woman beginning to fall for his charms as they carefully closed the gate and walked to the car.

'You'd be living there, would you?' the woman asked suddenly. 'Only we don't want more second home owners around here. The place is deserted for most of the year. Not nice at all. Like a ghost town.'

'Oh yes. Couldn't leave a delightful spot like this empty for long.'

'It's Major's who are selling it. Old couple who owned it died last year. I hate seeing it empty.' She walked down the slope to the beach, dragged along by her dog.

'I must have missed our wedding,' Bryher said with a giggle when they drove away. 'Was it a big affair?'

'Oh, massive. Half the county were there. You looked wonderful in a huge frothy, white creation. Your friends made an arch of honour with their surf boards and the bridesmaids all wore pink wet suits and bike helmets.'

'No wonder I missed it,' she laughed, 'All the same, not exactly honest, are you? I'm not happy about misleading people.'

'We got the name of the agent. Hope you made a note? Very promising little property. Now, lunch. Do you know anywhere decent around here?'

'There's a nice pub in the next village.'

'We can go somewhere a bit grander than a pub if you like.'

'A pub will be quicker. We haven't got far along the coast yet.'

'Good girl. I like your thinking.'

'Or maybe I'm hungry and have a good appetite.'

'I noticed before. Okay. Point the way.'

★　★　★

After a substantial roast lunch in the village they took a walk along the harbour. There were a lot of people walking around and there was a definite early holiday feel to the place. Pretty cottages lined the narrow roads, all renovated and extended to within inches of their lives.

'Not much left to do here. Everything is modernised,' Bryher remarked.

'No — look at that derelict old warehouse at the end of the road. That's a perfect spec.'

'But it's falling down,' Bryher observed. 'What would you use it for?'

'That, my dear, is a perfect site for a development of holiday flats. At least half a dozen, and if we could lease a section of the car park for the residents, we are well set. Pictures, please, and from as many angles as possible. I'll go and pose so we don't alert anyone. We can cut me out of the pictures later. Then I'll get some of you, so we look like holidaymakers.'

'In case you hadn't noticed, most people take pictures with the sea and the pretty cottages as a background.'

'Ah well, I'm never most people,' he told her. 'But go on, if you must. Me with the harbour wall.' He pulled a silly face as she snapped away.

He instructed her to make notes on the village. Several teashops, souvenir shops, a fish and chip shop, a couple of pubs and a small supermarket were carefully listed.

'Makes for a perfect place for holiday lets. Plenty going on. What's the surf like round on the shore side?'

'Not bad. It's a bit pebbly but it is possible.'

'See, you know everything about the area. You're definitely an asset. Nigel will surely approve of you.'

'Nigel?' she queried.

'My backer and business partner. You'll meet him next week. We're having our review. I'll need you working in the office tomorrow. Follow up on today's stuff. I have to work in St Ives in the afternoon but we'll get started on this first thing. Now, we'll make a start down the western side of the Lizard before we call it a day.'

★ ★ ★

When they finally arrived back at her cottage, Bryher felt quite weary but excited by what they'd seen and what she had learned about her new boss. There had been a good few laughs, as well as some serious research. She felt some apprehension about what she was taking on, feeling she knew too little about the work. She was slightly more comfortable with the idea of marketing, as her university course had covered some aspects. She arranged to be in the office at Tristan's house at eight-thirty the next day.

The answering machine was flashing. Her mother . . . as she had guessed it would be. The usual message, asking about work and why didn't she come home. She dialled the number, keen to tell her news.

'Hi Mum. Only me. Returning your call.'

'Hallo, darling. How are you? I hope you're not still struggling.'

'Struggling? Not at all. Guess what? I got a job.'

'Oh that's wonderful news. What is it?'

'Motorcycle courier,' Bryher teased. Well, it was partly true.

'Oh Bryher, how could you? You know how much I hate that wretched machine. Time you got yourself a nice little car. Daddy will help, you know he will. You could have a brand new one if you chose a suitable model. She's only got a job as bike courier,' her mother called to her father. 'Daddy is not pleased,' she was informed.

'Okay. Only joking. Though I have been working this week as a courier. One of my clients was so impressed, he offered me a job as a sort of personal assistant.' *Might as well big it up*, Bryher thought.

'Oh darling, that's wonderful. Much more sensible. About this car. If you've got a respectable job, you really need a decent car.'

'Please Mum, stop trying to organise my life. If you must know, my boss is also a motorbike enthusiast.'

'Oh!' came the disappointed response.

'So what does he do when he isn't cycling round the countryside?'

'He's an accountant.'

'Oh, that's wonderful. She's personal assistant to an accountant. Isn't that splendid? Daddy thinks it's splendid. And he agrees about the car.'

'Thanks very much. I'll think about it.' It was easier than arguing. 'So tell me what you've been doing.'

The conversation ran on. Daddy was working too hard. Martin and the children had been over and various friends had been seen and had asked after Bryher.

'So, when are you coming to see us? You haven't been here since Christmas.'

'Soon, Mum. But I need to settle into my new job. See exactly what it entails. Actually, Tristan is more than an accountant. He runs a property development business. As a matter of fact, we've been out today doing a sort of scouting trip. It should be fun.'

'And is he nice, this Tristan? What sort of age?'

'Maybe thirtyish. And yes, he's very nice.'

'Married?'

'No, he's not.'

'About time you started going out with someone a bit more sensible than your surfing and biking crowd.'

'Mum! I am not going out with him. Well — not apart from work trips.'

'I see.'

'What do you mean by 'I see' in that tone of voice?'

'Nothing. I think you do like him. You're rather quick to defend him. Well, I'm delighted you've got something sensible to do. Good luck and don't forget you promised to come and see us soon.'

'I won't, Mum. Love you both. Bye.'

She opened the microwave to thaw bread for a sandwich. There was a really bad smell. The fish pie she'd put in days ago was still sitting there.

'I must get myself sorted,' she said aloud. She grabbed an old carrier bag and tipped the pie into it, tying it firmly and dumping it in the bin. How could she have left it there for so long? New job, new start and a more organised lifestyle beckoned.

All the same, a ride along the bypass at six o'clock tomorrow was definitely a must. She couldn't give up all of her old life just yet.

5

It was raining hard when Bryher awoke the next morning. Something was blowing around in the garden. It was not a morning for speeding along on her bike, with a crosswind like this. The breakers were huge on the beach and she was tempted to grab her board and go for an exciting ride. But it would leave her a very short time to get to her new job.

'Oh dear,' she muttered to her old, battered teddy who sat near her bed. 'I think I am becoming more common-sensical. Maybe it's time to grow up after all.' She sighed, thinking that any moment she might seriously consider her parents' offer of a loan to buy a car.

The next hurdle was what to wear. 'It's so easy for a bloke. His biggest decision is which tie to wear with the suit.' Teddy made no comment.

She decided that some of her smarter trousers would have to do, and maybe a button-through shirt rather than a T-shirt. Once she had more money, she must do something about her wardrobe.

Promptly at eight twenty-five, she parked her bike in front of Tristan's house and walked round the side, assuming correctly that the converted summerhouse was at the back. His house was a red brick building, not at all typical of Cornwall. Fortunately the rain had stopped.

She knocked on the door and pushed it open. The summerhouse was massive — more of a live-in chalet, and had a tiny kitchen area as well as a small bathroom. It meant the place was quite independent of the house and perfect as an office.

'Morning,' Bryher called.

'Oh, hi there,' Tristan replied, crawling out from under his desk. 'I was trying to work out how we could put in a simple network. I've got a laptop you can use, but we'll need you to have access to some of the files. I also need you to get us organised with a coffee machine and toaster, and one of those little fridge things. I'd like us to start the day with a working breakfast, then we can begin at eight. Gives us time to meet each morning and discuss what we need to do, before I go to the office on some days. Is that all right with you? There's a kettle and instant coffee for now.'

Bryher laughed. 'Sounds as if you're putting the important things first. There's a slight problem, I can't carry stuff like that on my bike. But don't feel you have to feed me all the time. I think we've done more eating together than anything else.' She paused. 'So, what's the agenda today?'

'I'd like you to set up a viewing for that cottage we saw. Tomorrow would suit me. Morning. Check on the warehouse, too. That may be more difficult. You may need to go over there and ask around. Try land registry. I have an account with them so you'll need the number — oh, and my credit card number for searches.'

'You'll trust me with your card?'

'Of course. It's the business card. I'll give you the details you need. Can you drive, by the way? Apart from the bike, I mean. You'd better take the car for shopping; there'll be other stuff too. Nigel's confirmed he's good for Thursday, by the way. He'll meet us here at nine, so there will be stuff to prepare for that. Reports on what we saw yesterday.'

'Okay. Where shall I sit? I can drive but, as I said, I don't have a car.'

'I need to organise a desk for you. This is all happening a bit suddenly and I haven't got it sorted yet. I've got a spare table in the house. You'll have to make do with that for now — and the laptop. We'll maybe have a shopping expedition tomorrow, when we view the property.'

'If we *can* view tomorrow.'

'You'll have to organise it. Don't take

no for an answer.'

'No, boss. Three bags full, boss.'

He gave her a grin. 'I may not be the easiest person to work for but I'm sure you can handle my impatience and bad temper.'

He gave her his most winning smile. Her heart gave a twist and she did her best to push away the romantic feelings she was developing for him. Work and pleasure could not mix. Tristan may be the best thing she had encountered for a long time, but this had to be a working, completely professional relationship. However hard that might be. The thought of him in his wet suit, and then in his swimming trunks, crept into her mind. She blushed and pushed it out again.

The morning flew by. Tristan showed her the various programmes they would use on the computer; lists of properties, builders and a mass of people she would need to contact at times, all of whose details were housed in a bulging filing cabinet.

'Needs sorting out, really, doesn't it?' he admitted when he saw her expression. 'Yet another job for Super-girl.'

Working from a slightly wobbly folding table and an elderly laptop computer, Bryher came to the conclusion that it might have been better to start the job a week later so that everything could have been prepared in advance. She needed a proper desk and a telephone for her own use, not a shared one with Tristan. When he went to his other job in the afternoon, she worked at his desk and achieved most of the tasks she had been set. Eventually, she managed to get through to the agent about the cottage.

'I'm sorry, we don't have anyone available to show you round tomorrow. End of the week any good?' The person in the office was most unhelpful.

'And does the vendor know this?' Bryher asked. 'That you only have such limited viewing possibilities?'

'I'm sorry, madam, I don't know what you mean.'

'Does the vendor know you are unable to show a possible keen buyer round the property except for one day a week? I'd have thought the competition to make a sale would make you very enthusiastic to organise viewings when requested. We will look at the cottage tomorrow if you can arrange it. Otherwise, forget it. I have a contact who will easily make it known to the vendor that you have such a poor service.' She crossed her fingers, thinking of the dog-walking lady who had accosted them.

'Leave it with me, madam. I'll see what I can arrange. Can I have your number, please? I'll call you back.'

Bryher gave a smile of triumph and then realised she didn't actually know the phone number. Thinking quickly, she gave her own mobile number and her own name. Ten minutes later, the woman called back with an appointment for ten o'clock the next morning. She was rather curt. But so what? Bryher had achieved her appointment.

It was a great relief that she wouldn't have to explain to Tristan that she had failed.

At five o'clock, she decided to call it a day. She had no idea what time Tristan would be back, but she had nothing else to do. She left him a note and locked the door behind her. As the door locked itself automatically, she hoped he had another key somewhere. Something else to add to her growing list of things to discuss and organise.

After the wet beginning, the day had turned into quite a pleasant one. She saw several surfers out in the bay when she got home and couldn't resist joining them. She couldn't live in a more convenient place, she thought. Home from work. Straight into a wet suit and down to the beach. Paradise. She knew a few of the surfers, and chatted with them as they lay on their boards, waiting for the big wave that made the sport worthwhile. It was a long wait. Conditions were rather choppy.

'So how's the new job?' Bill yelled.

'Okay, I think,' she yelled back.

'Boss not surfing with you today?'

'Think he'll be a weekend surfer. Think I'm going in now. One more wave and that's me done for the day.'

Bill raised his hand, nodded and then pointed behind him. She turned and saw a huge wave approaching. They were in the perfect spot to catch it just before it broke and they rode in side by side, whooping with the excitement of it. They both managed to stay upright right to the shallows and slapped their hands together in a high five as they reached the beach.

'Worth the wait after all,' Bryher called.

'You're pretty good for a girl. You should enter the competition.'

'No way. I've got enough on my plate at the moment.'

'You going to make a coffee for me?' Bill asked.

'I guess so.'

After an hour of his light-hearted chat, Bryher sent him on his way.

'Things to do,' she told him.

'You're getting much too serious, young lady. Don't let the world of work spoil you completely.'

'As if. Now, scoot.'

After he had left, she began to sort out her wardrobe. She needed a good clear out and some new clothes, more suitable for her new role in life. There would be times when jeans, even smart jeans, just would not do. Soon she had a heap ready for the charity shop, a heap to bin and a rather smaller heap that might do for work. The ironing board came out, and pressed items were carefully hung in the now spacious wardrobe. The trouble with biking to work was that she had to wear her leathers, and anything beneath would be crushed. Nor could she carry much on her bike box without it being creased. Perhaps she needed to take up her parents' offer of a car.

★ ★ ★

At six o'clock the next morning, Bryher took the bike for a run along the bypass. Only slightly exceeding the speed limit, she spotted the red-helmeted rider just ahead of her. She accelerated and caught him up, winning a wave from him as she sped by. He caught her up and together they raced for the roundabout. Neck and neck, they reached it and drove round for a re-run. She let him get ahead, then raced after him.

On the other carriageway, a police car was flashing blue lights. Instinctively both slowed down and went sedately towards the roundabout at the other end of the bypass.

Tristan pulled into the layby on the side road and unhooked his helmet. She stopped alongside him.

'That was close,' he said with a laugh.

'Don't think they were flashing for us. They went right on towards Penzance. Think we call that a draw.'

'You going to have breakfast?' he asked. 'Only I haven't got the coffee machine or toaster yet.'

'Follow me home if you like. I've still got the odd few slices of bread left.'

Over breakfast, they discussed the day's plans.

'I'd like to do some shopping this morning after the viewing. I need to sort out the office. Get you a desk and another phone for starters.'

'Great. I gave my mobile number to the estate agent, and my name too. Don't quite know what I was thinking.'

'No, that's good. They won't associate my name as a property developer and we can continue as a married couple and get the price down. Once they sniff a developer, they won't drop the price.'

'Not exactly honest, is it?' she said again.

'Dog-eat-dog world. Right. I'll see you soon. Oh, remind me to give you a key to the office. You need to be able to get in when I'm not there.'

★　★　★

'It's a delightful property,' the estate agent began. 'Needs a bit of work of course, but it was owned by an elderly couple who clearly loved it. The vendors, family members, are of course reluctant to sell but needs must.'

'How long has it been on the market? I can look it up, of course.'

'Nine months. There are planning restrictions. It's a very old property.'

They looked round the pretty, old cottage. Tristan was non-committal and Bryher took the lead from him. At the end of the visit, the agent asked anxiously what they had thought.

'It's a rather high price for so small a property. We couldn't offer anything close to the asking price.'

'Well, I can always put an offer forward,' the agent said encouragingly.

'We'll think about it. Thanks for showing us round.'

'I'll give you some time to think and then call you again.'

They left, with Bryher having little idea of Tristan's thoughts on the property. She asked him.

'Nice place, but not much money in it from a development view. Need a twenty-five percent drop in the price before I'd be interested. Nice spot, though. I'd quite like to live there myself. Handy for surfing as well.'

'You'd be that keen on surfing?'

'Maybe. The outbuilding would make a good office. What d'you think?'

'I'd be very happy working there. Especially in summer. Quick dash down to the beach in my lunch hour. Yes, definite possibilities. But I thought this was a business proposition?'

'Like I say, not much profit in it. I'll leave it for now. If it hangs around, I'll make a reduced offer sometime in the future, maybe.'

'So, if the woman rings back, I'll say we decided against?'

'That's it. Now, let's go and buy things. Desk, coffee machine and toaster. And a little fridge. Where do we go for bargains?'

She led him to a large DIY store and

they found most things they needed. It was fun and Bryher pinched herself, realising this was supposed to be work.

They put together the flat-pack desk, arguing about which piece went where. 'They say a child can do it, so why don't they supply the child?' she asked in frustration, as it fell apart for a second time. Eventually, it was all set up and, rather late in the day, they were ready for work. Tristan had a long agenda of his own and so Bryher was left to try and track down the owners of the old warehouse they had seen.

'Do you think it's worth asking round in person?' she suggested. 'I'm not even sure what it's called, to type anything into the land registry site.'

'Could do. Local shops and the pub might know. Try them tomorrow. I'm at the office for most of the day so you'll have to do it on your own. I've also made a list for you. We need reports doing ready for Thursday, and Nigel.'

'I might need a bit of direction for that.'

'No problem.'

The rest of the afternoon was spent sorting out various requirements and going through the files for Bryher to familiarise herself with the various projects on the books. She was surprised by the extent of the work that was going on and she looked with new admiration at the man at the next desk. His rather casual attitude belied the amount of work he had been doing since he began his business.

Her list for the next day was formidable, but she was determined that Tristan would be pleased with her. She planned an early start tomorrow.

'Don't forget to give me a key,' she remembered just as she was leaving. 'If you're not here, I shall be stuck outside.'

'I'd forgotten. Good job you didn't.'

★   ★   ★

At just before eight next day, she arrived at Tristan's house. He was already working and there was fresh coffee made.

'Didn't expect to see you here,' Bryher remarked in surprise.

'I wanted to be sure everything was ready for you to work on during the day. You can always send me a text if you need to ask anything, but don't phone. I may be with a client.'

'I did some shopping last night.' She took out coffee, bread, butter and spreads. 'Oh! I forgot milk. But you drink coffee black, don't you?'

He nodded. 'Let me know what you spent. Did you keep the receipt? If we have receipts, it's all so much easier.'

'Oh, for goodness' sake. It wasn't much. And I'll be eating some of it.'

'My turn for the next lot, then. Better get on. I have to leave before nine.'

He was very efficient, with careful instructions typed out ready for her. This was more like her expectations of an accountant. Biking and surfing couldn't have been further away. All the same, her thoughts drifted to the muscular body that she knew lay beneath the smart business suit and immaculate shirt and tie. She wondered who did his laundry for him. She knew she couldn't iron so beautifully neatly. Her collars always had those tiny wrinkles and in the corners where the buttons fastened.

She dragged her thoughts back: Why should she worry about his ironing? She would never have to do it and a man like Tristan would never be seriously interested in anyone like her.

'So, what do you think?' he was asking.

'Sorry. I drifted for a moment.' He looked cross. 'I was just planning my order of work for today. I'll go to make enquiries about the warehouse later in the day. Maybe I could get lunch and start a casual conversation.'

'Leave that to you. I was asking about the reports. We'll need three copies, so make sure you can use the printer. It's pretty straightforward. Here's the company credit card for you to use with land registry. The password is on the list I gave you. Okay? You're on your own now. I may be back by five, but lock up if you need to leave earlier.' He swept out of the office, leaving the place feeling empty and not a little lonely.

6

Feeling slightly uncertain about what she was doing, Bryher worked through Tristan's list. The phone rang. She bit her lip. She hadn't asked him how he liked it to be answered. Did she use the company name or not? He usually gave his own name, so she did the same.

'Bryher speaking,' she announced.

'Is Tristan there?'

'I'm afraid he's out. Who's calling? Can I take a message?'

'It's Nigel speaking. You must be the new girl. We'll meet tomorrow. Is he at the St Ives office?'

'He's working there today, yes.'

'Fine. I'll call him there.' He put the phone down and Bryher frowned. Tristan did not want to be disturbed, but she could do nothing about it. She gave a shrug and continued her work.

At midday, she left the office and

rode into Porthtroon, the village where the old warehouse was situated. She wanted to succeed in finding out the owner and to see if it might be for sale. The Land Registry had yielded nothing. This possibly meant it wasn't actually registered, she had learned. It had not been on the market for many years. Encouraging, she thought.

She ordered a sandwich at the little pub, and a coffee. She sat at the bar, hoping to engage the barman in conversation. It took some time before she could get round to the old building.

'Quite spoils the look of the whole village, doesn't it?' she suggested.

'Be nice if it could be tidied up. Someone was talking about it being turned back into a fish wholesale place, but I don't see it myself. Most of the fishing boats around here are used for holiday trips nowadays. The whole industry has gone belly-up in recent years.' Once the barman got going, it was hard to stop him. His family had been fishermen, it seemed.

'So, who owns it, do you know?'

'Some old boy who's gone up-country to live with his daughter.'

'So it's just been left to fall to pieces? Sad.'

'Just an old eyesore these days. There's someone who might know. Jasper? Here a mo. This young lady is asking about the old warehouse. You know who owns it?'

'Be old Wesley's family. They do live out of the county now. You interested in 'im?'

Bryher's heart began to thump. She took a deep breath to steady herself and spoke as casually as she could.

'Not really. I was just thinking it spoilt the look of such a pretty village.'

'You'm right, gal. Reckon the council should do summat. Wants torchin' if you asks me.'

'So where does this Wesley live?'

'I 'ad a card from him last Christmas. Gloucester way, I do think.'

'You know his other name?'

'Wesley Timms.'

'Really? That was my mother's name. I wonder if we could be related.'

'Lot of Timms do live around here.'

'Can I buy you a drink?' Bryher offered. That might get him talking more.

'Ta. Good of you. Not often a young lady offers to buy for an old codger.'

Almost an hour later, Bryher had got a few more details and was anxious to get back to her computer to do some more searching. Intriguing that she almost shared a name with the owner. It wasn't impossible that they could be distant relatives, but she didn't really think that was worth pursuing. She might call her mother and ask if they knew of any relatives but meanwhile, she could do some searches using the computer.

She soon had a couple of possible addresses and phone numbers, but decided to wait for Tristan's approval before making contact. She had throughly enjoyed her detective work and decided to wait until he came back to the office so she could share her news.

'You're still here,' Tristan said with some surprise. 'I thought you'd be long gone. Nothing wrong, is there?'

'I just thought I'd wait. I think I've done everything for tomorrow.'

He flicked through the typed sheets she had prepared and nodded approval. 'Did you get time to do some research on the Porthtroon place?'

She told him about her efforts and he grinned.

'See? I told you my instincts are never wrong. Well done! Have you tried phoning either of the possible contacts you found?'

'I thought I should wait for you to do that. I don't want to make any mistakes that might jeopardise anything.'

'Let's give it a try now.'

She sat at her desk while he phoned.

'I'm sorry to trouble you but I'm trying to locate a Wesley Timms. Have I got the correct number?' He paused for a moment as he listened. 'Thank you.

Again, my apologies for troubling you.' He put the phone down and pulled a face. 'Not that one. Try again.'

He repeated the same pattern and this time, made a thumbs-up sign. He continued. 'I understand you may be the owner of an almost derelict warehouse building in Porthtroon? I have heard that the council are considering making a compulsory purchase on the property, just to tidy it up.' Another pause. 'It's a rumour, of course, but there maybe some truth in it. I was wondering if you'd thought of trying to sell it? The council rarely pay the true value, as you might expect. I'd be prepared to make you an offer, once I've looked over it, that is.

You would? Excellent. You'll actually come down? Can I give you my phone number?'

When he hung up, Tristan was jubilant. He grabbed Bryher's hands and danced her round the room. She collapsed back onto her chair, laughing.

'Well done. Mr Timms is willing to

consider selling. He'll arrange to come down soon and we can have a meeting. Now, we need to make a preliminary planning enquiry.'

'Isn't that jumping the gun a bit?'

'Not if it's just an inquiry. It will affect the eventual price anyway.'

He explained yet more of the intricacies of property ownership to her and finally looked at his watch. 'What are you doing for supper?'

'Haven't thought yet.'

'Let's go and eat at the pub. Bit of a celebration.'

'I still think you're getting ahead of yourself.'

'So what? I feel good. Nigel's going to be delighted.'

'Okay, then thank you. I'd like to.'

'I'll just go and put on something more comfortable. Come and see the house. Nothing special. Typical bachelor place with no nice touches to make it homely. Never enough time.'

As he had said, Tristan's home was rather uninspiring. The living room was mostly brown, functional but with no splashes of colour to relieve it.

'Grab yourself a drink while I change. There's wine or beer in the fridge.'

'Thanks,' Bryher replied. 'I'll wait till we get to the pub. I have to ride the bike back.'

'I'll drop you back home. Leave the bike here.'

'And how do I get to work tomorrow? I could go back home and change, myself.'

'You're fine. I just don't like going out in the business suit.'

'And mine isn't a business suit, of course.'

'Come on. You know what I mean. You dress exactly right for you.'

'That sounds a bit of a back-handed compliment. Let's not get into any deeper waters.'

★ ★ ★

After their meal, he drove them back to his home.

'You could always stay over if you like. Then you've no excuse for being late in the morning.'

She stared at him, utterly shocked at the sudden, coolly-made offer.

'What exactly are you saying?' she murmured, her heart racing and her mind suddenly turning to what felt like thick porridge.

'Well, nothing sinister. Not that I'm not tempted, of course, but I do have a spare room. That's what I was really saying.' He smiled and once more, her heart skipped a beat or several. 'Then we can open a rather nice bottle of wine I've been saving for a special occasion.'

'And this is a special occasion?'

'Actually, yes. You'd be my first guest.'

'I don't have anything with me. No change of clothes. No toothbrush.'

'I've got new toothbrushes but I can't help with clothes. Just an idea.'

'Well, thanks. It's a nice idea but not very practical.'

'Don't you trust me?'

'Of course I trust you. I'm just not

sure about myself.'

'Is that an admission that you find me attractive?'

Bryher's blush deepened. She considered herself practically head over heels in love with him — not that she wanted to admit it, even to herself.

'Of course you're an attractive man,' she mumbled. 'You know you are.'

His eyes drew hers with a compelling gaze. 'I don't, actually. I'm not as full of confidence as you might think. Well, if you won't stay, I suggest you get on your way before I can't let you go.'

'We've hardly known each other for any time,' she ventured, not really wanting to let this conversation end. 'It's only been a week or so. However tempting your offer, I don't want to rush things any more than we already have. Heavens, in just a few days, I'm working for you, we've eaten out together four or five times. Breakfast together every day.'

'You're absolutely right. But honestly, I didn't have any ulterior motives.'

'I'm sure you didn't. But after a bottle of wine, and it being late already, who knows what might happen?'

His lips brushed hers. 'I'll see you in the morning. Drive safely.'

He watched her leave. Would they have a future together? He pulled himself together. As she had said, it was early days and they didn't really know each other well. All the same, he realised he had never felt quite like this about anyone before.

As Bryher drove home, she kept wishing she had taken up the offer to stay over. She would have seen another side to Tristan. So far, most of the things they had done together had been rather superficial. But her head had returned to some sort of sanity, and she knew she was doing the right thing.

His gentle kiss as they were parting had left her weak at the knees. It was truly little more than a kiss between friends, but it made her realise there was going to be a lot more to the future, if he became a greater part of it.

★ ★ ★

Bryher felt slightly apprehensive about meeting Tristan's partner the next day. She had no idea of his age, or what he was like. The few words he had spoken on the phone suggested he was fairly brusque, but that may not have been typical. Though she was early, she'd scarcely unzipped her leathers when he arrived.

'Another biker?' he observed in a slightly derogatory tone. He held out his hand. 'Nigel Western.' Struggling out of her boots, she shook his hand.

'Bryher Jenkins.' She felt as if she were under scrutiny and hesitated before offering to make coffee. Tristan nodded to her to go ahead and she set to work, listening carefully to the two men's conversation. There was little in the way of small talk and they seemed to get down to business very quickly. Nigel was older than Tristan, possibly in his late fifties, and quite an attractive man. He gave away little about his background or how he had made his money but clearly he had quite a large fortune behind him.

'Looks like you've made a decent start,' he told Bryher, when Tristan explained about the properties they had seen. 'Pursue the warehouse. I like that one. The cottage isn't worth it.'

'I might look again for my own use,' Tristan told him. 'But if I can put it through the books, I can minimise VAT. If I can get it cheaply enough.'

'Of course. Update me on the craft unit project.'

Bryher wasn't quite clear on this particular project and listened carefully, jotting down notes as the two men spoke. She was mentally adding up the financial commitment involved as they were talking, and gasped. It was a massive amount of money in her eyes. It put both of them in an entirely different league. What was she thinking about, even considering that she and Tristan could have any sort of future relationship?

At eleven o'clock, just as she was about to offer more coffee, Nigel closed the files and put them into his briefcase.

'Thanks, both of you. Must go and collect Andrea from the hairdresser's. My life won't be worth living if I'm late. Welcome aboard, Bryher. I think you'll be good for us. Maybe you should think about losing the bike. Not a good image for us.'

'I'll think about it, when I've saved up a bit. But at least it makes me look as if I don't have a fortune to spend. Could help keep costs down.' She was slightly tongue in cheek as she spoke.

'Maybe. But he's quite mad enough for one company. Don't want you racing around the county trying to be competitive.' The two bike enthusiasts looked at each other and smiled knowingly.

'I'm sure you needn't worry. Shall I organise a car for Bryher, then?'

She gasped, having thought they were expecting her to buy her own car.

'Think you should. Reasonably modest,

though; keep up the suggestion we don't have unlimited funds. Till next month, then. Keep me updated.'

'Thanks, Nigel. I'll email details of the next prospects.' Tristan escorted him back to his car, a very large and expensive model, while Bryher cleared away the coffee cups. She looked up as he returned.

'Thanks for the promise of a car. He's quite a powerhouse, isn't he?'

'Doesn't suffer fools gladly. But you made a good impression.'

'Didn't think I said enough to be noticed.'

'He liked the fact you weren't constantly asking or interrupting.'

'So, what's his background?'

'He's taken early retirement. He owned a financial investment company. Sold out well before the crash and made a packet. A massive packet, actually. This is more or less a hobby to him. Gives him an interest and hopefully, will make him even more money. He likes to know what's going on but doesn't like to be too involved. This is where I come in.

We're partners but it's his capital that mainly funds the projects.

'So — he wants you to have a car. Any thoughts?'

'My parents will be delighted. But, I can't part with the bike. Not yet.'

'Soulmates in that, at least. I could never part with mine, either. Can't have you racing with anyone else along the bypass. So, what do you fancy?'

'You know something? I've never actually given much thought to makes of car. You suggest something.'

'I'll pick up some brochures.' He named a price range and she raised an eyebrow. 'That's more than you were offering as an annual salary.'

'We can review that as we move on. Depends how useful you are. But if you have a decent small car, it's down as a company asset. And you can get around without needing a complete change of clothes every time.'

There was always plenty of work to keep Bryher occupied and she soon evolved her own routine. The days that

Tristan worked as an accountant in St Ives were quite flexible. He was coming to rely on her more and more and she was loving it. They ate out together once a week, and he came surfing on a couple of occasions. She had a small, bright yellow car which she used every day.

'You're becoming so *respectable*,' her friend Bill told her. 'You haven't been out for a drink with us for weeks.'

'I know. Saturday evening, I promise. Just been really busy.'

'And this flash new car of yours. Bit up-market, isn't it?'

'I know. But at least it's yellow. Not a nice safe grey or something.'

★   ★   ★

She never made it for the promised drink. On Saturday morning, Tristan called and asked her to join him at the office. It seemed Mr Wesley Timms had decided to visit at very short notice.

'I'd like you here so we can chat him up a bit. Wear jeans and be casual. And bring your bike. Looks better than having a smart new-looking car.'

Bryher obeyed, but was beginning to feel they were being rather deceitful. She didn't like the idea that they might be trying to cheat the old man. She voiced her opinion to Tristan but he was unsympathetic.

'We have to get the best deal we can. Whatever we offer will probably be a whole lot more than he would expect. It's only the land we're buying, after all. And there's the expense of pulling down the old building and getting rid of materials that may cost a lot for disposal.'

'All the same . . . ' She sighed. 'Okay. You're the boss.'

'Good girl. Now, I said we'd meet him at the site at eleven.'

'So he won't even know I've got a company car.'

'True. I wasn't thinking it through.'

They drove down to Porthtroon, parked in the general car park and wandered down to the warehouse. Tristan walked round, prodding the walls to see if there was loose stone. Moments later, they saw an elderly man approaching. He had a shock of white hair and a well-tanned face, his eyes sunken after a lifetime of squinting into the sun. He was probably in his late seventies, Bryher thought. He was accompanied by a younger man of a similar build with fairish hair, whom they took to be his son.

'Mr Timms? I'm Tristan Adams. This is my colleague, Bryher Jenkins. Nice to meet you. Thank you again for coming down.' They all shook hands.

'This is my lad.' The son stepped forward and shook hands, grimacing at being called a lad. 'Named for the island, are you?' he asked Bryher.

'Yes. My parents went there for their honeymoon.'

He seemed to lose interest as he turned to look at his building.

'Old place is looking a bit sad. Always hoped my lad would be interested in the fishing and make use of it in some way.'

'Now, Dad, it's all been said. No

money in fishing any more since all the regulations came in. Besides, my work is up-country now.'

'All the same, smelling the sea again makes me feel homesick. Reckon I made a mistake, moving away.'

'Come, now, Dad. You know you couldn't manage on your own.'

The pale, rheumy eyes stared wistfully down the harbour road and Bryher felt quite emotional. It was just how she would feel if she had to move away.

'So what did you use the old buildings for?' she asked him gently.

'Bit of carpentry during the winter months. And stored me nets in there. But, as my boy says, that's all over. I expect you'll be wanting a look round.'

He pulled a bunch of keys from his pocket and searched among them for the one that would open the rickety door. With great difficulty, he pushed it open. It was dark, dusty and filled with rubbish. Bryher could see Tristan calculating the cost of shifting all the debris.

'So what do you reckon you'd do with this lot?' the old man asked.

'I'm not sure. Maybe open up some sort of business. Turn it into small units for shops. Haven't really thought it through.' Tristan was being very non-committal at this stage. He was testing the ground, not wanting to say anything Mr Timms might object to.

'Don't want any of them prissy little holiday houses on the site,' Mr Timms remarked.

'There are lots of holiday lets in the village already,' Tristan commented.

No-one could dispute that, but Bryher still felt he was guilty of being slightly dishonest and was slightly uncomfortable.

'Had a letter from the council, tellin' me to tidy the place up. Folks round here been complaining. Says it's an eyesore. You got to me just at the right time. So, what do you think? You interested or shall I let the council have it?'

'I'm interested, but it depends how

much you want for it,' Tristan replied.

'Make me an offer and I'll let you know if you're close.'

'Let's go and get a drink at the pub and we can discuss it.'

7

Mr Timms junior looked as if he was ready for battle. It was not going to be a pushover between Tristan and the older man. Bryher collected the drinks and came to sit beside Tristan, and the sparring began.

Tristan wrote his opening price on a piece of paper. It seemed this was the traditional way of dealing among some of the older Cornishmen.

Wesley shook his head and wrote his figure on the paper. Tristan crossed it out and made a new offer. The paper went back and forth for some time and, without a word being spoken, suddenly an agreement was reached.

The son looked at the agreed price and nodded. He had remained silent throughout the negotiations, clearly knowing he would not be allowed to intervene before approval was reached.

The men all shook hands. Bryher sat there, feeling somewhat left out.

'Shall I get some more drinks? To seal the deal?' she offered. Tristan agreed and she went to the bar.

'You got a solicitor?' Mr Timms asked.

'I have.' Tristan took out a sheet of paper from his briefcase with the solicitor's name and address on it, together with his own details.

'I'll get my chap to write to him and we'll set the ball rolling. Pasties all round,' Wesley said firmly and pushed his son to go and buy them. Clearly it was his way of cementing the deal.

It was almost two o'clock by the time they got away. Tristan seemed pleased, but Bryher was quite shocked when he told her the final price they had agreed for the property.

'And that still makes a viable project, does it?'

'Certainly. I'd have paid considerably more. But he was happy enough.'

'Don't you feel guilty, then? He

might have needed the extra money.'

'Why should I feel guilty? He was happy with the price. It was fair enough. Now he can move on. Forget about it.'

'But he specifically said he didn't want — what was it? *Prissy little holiday houses*. Isn't that exactly what you're planning?'

'Come on now, Bryher. We're a business. If we have to bend the truth a bit at times, that's the deal.'

'Like pretending we were married at that cottage?' She grimaced slightly as she recalled the deception. 'Did you hear any more of that, by the way?'

'I emailed the agent and said I'd only consider it if they'd accept a much lower price. I never heard again. Fancy a drive round again? We never finished driving round the Lizard. You busy for the rest of the day?'

'Not particularly. Okay, if you want to. But haven't you got enough on your plate already?'

'I've got a wonderful new assistant who takes most of the load off my shoulders. Only suggesting we look.'

'Fine. Nice day for a drive. But I'd have brought a camera if I'd known.'

'I've got everything we need in the back. Be prepared, I say.'

'You'd got this planned, hadn't you?'

'I thought it might be an idea that could work.'

'You certainly expect to get your money's worth out of me, don't you?'

'Your hours are negotiable. Nothing in your contract to say you can't work on Saturdays.'

'And what contract would that be?'

He smiled. 'Fair comment. We'll organise something. But for now, I thought you might have enjoyed my company as well. We could, if you like, just be going on a date. Nice drive. Cosy evening meal somewhere special.'

'And is that what you're planning?'

'Could be. If you'd like to. Don't you enjoy my company?'

She felt herself quiver under his gaze. 'Of course. You know I do.'

'And I'd hardly be asking you out on

a Saturday if I didn't enjoy yours. So, relax and enjoy yourself. Now, I saw there was something for sale along this road. Let's see where it is.'

''Relax', did you say? Impossible with you in this mood.'

'I'm excited by the deal we've just done. Nigel will be delighted. Thanks for your help.'

'I hardly did anything.'

'But your presence definitely helped. Having an attractive woman always helps oil the wheels.'

'Now hang on. I'm not some fashion accessory designed to smooth things over.' Bryher was suddenly angry. She hated the thought of anyone treating her as some sort of lesser being, just because she was female.

'Hey, don't be so sensitive. I was teasing. It's your business skills I love about you. You get straight to the heart of everything and do it in a way that doesn't upset people. I'm too brusque at times, I know — and you provide the perfect foil.'

'Excuse me. Did you say it's something you *love* about me?'

'I believe I did. Not a problem, is it?'

She felt herself blushing. Her emotions seemed to be out of control.

'Did you actually mean love? It's a very big word.'

He turned off the road and pulled up in a farm gateway. She looked around for a sale board, but Tristan leaned over and took her hand.

'Bryher. I've really come to appreciate your special qualities. You are a very unusual woman, as well as a most attractive one. Working with you over the past weeks has made me realise just how lonely my life had been. I've always put my work first. I know I'm driven in very many ways and I'll probably never really change. So, whatever the word love really means, there are indeed many things I love about you.'

'I see. But that doesn't mean you love me?'

His hand tightened on hers. 'I'm not sure. I think I might do.'

'Oh, fine. Don't push yourself, will you? Let's get on.'

She felt annoyed. Just when she thought they might be getting closer, he was sending out mixed messages.

He stared at her, his grip preventing her pulling her hand away. His dark eyes held a troubled look. Bryher endeavoured to control her emotions. A minute earlier, she had felt herself flying; now she felt totally flattened.

'I'm sorry. I've upset you. I am very fond of you, and I admire you very much. Please forgive my clumsy speech. I wasn't trying to hurt you in any way. I suppose I shouldn't have used the word 'love' in such a cavalier way.

'The trouble is, with our language, we have just the one word for love. I can 'love' apple pie. Fine. I can 'love' my dog. Also fine. I can say 'I love you' and a whole huge well of emotions suddenly rises. The way I was using the word was, I suppose, rather too casual for you. And I think I'd better stop now before I drown in my own words.'

'Definitely. Don't dig yourself in any deeper. Let's look for your property before one of us says something we shouldn't.'

It was something of a fruitless afternoon, and they were treating each other with a degree of caution after the earlier conversation. Tristan saw a sign to Kynance Cove and turned off the road suddenly.

'Where are you going? There's nothing down there likely to be for sale. It's all National Trust property.'

'Thought we might have a walk and clear our heads. I don't like that we have an atmosphere between us.' He grabbed some coins from the tray in the car to pay the parking fee and they climbed out.

'I love it here,' Bryher murmured. Haven't been for ages.'

'I don't think I've ever been. I take it there isn't much surf here, if you haven't been for a while?'

'Not the best. But it's very lovely.'

They walked down the steep path to

the beach. The pink thrift was making colourful patches among the grass. The late afternoon sun was shining and the sea a perfect blue. People on the beach were beginning to collect up the paraphernalia seemingly essential for a day out in these times.

'You know, I never remember having to carry so many things to the beach when we were kids,' Bryher remarked. 'Bucket, spade and a towel, that was it. Now it's tents, chairs, windbreaks, cold boxes and vast bags of clothes. Not to mention the body boards and wet suits.'

'I wouldn't fancy having to carry it all back up that hill to the car park. Ah, I see they have wheeled trolley things. That's today's family for you.'

They strolled along the beach and into the openings and caves that lined the shore there.

'The tide's coming in, so we'd better not go too far. This whole area gets covered and it can come in quite fast — ' Tristan stopped and stared at her.

'What's the matter?' she asked, her heart hammering.

He seized her hands. 'I hope I haven't spoilt things. Between us. I've never felt like this about anyone before. When you were angry with me, I felt annoyed at first. Now I can't bear it. The days I go to St Ives to work, I miss you. Now, seeing you here, clearly loving the place, the sea, the beach and everything around us, I realise what has been missing in my life. I think I do actually love you. The thought of not having you in my life is something I can't contemplate. Do you think that's what love is?'

She stood staring back at him. There was a large lump in her throat blocking any words trying to come out. She had once speculated that she was falling head over heels in love with Tristan. But now she was here, with him so close, she was unbelievably nervous.

'I . . . I think it might be. Sorry, this is all a bit sudden.' Her voice didn't sound like hers, and her mouth was dry.

'I'm sorry. I shouldn't have said anything. I'm clearly no use with words with any sort of romantic context. Come on, we should move. That water's getting closer.' He almost dragged her along the rapidly narrowing strip of sand, glancing nervously seawards.

'It's going to be a case of paddling for it, I reckon.' Leaning on a rock, they pulled off shoes and socks and rolled up their trousers. 'Come on,' he yelled, grabbing her hand again, splashing along the fringes of the beach.

Laughing, they arrived at the top end of the beach just before the waves reached them. They climbed back up the steep path and put their shoes back on. Tristan pointed at the spot where they'd been minutes before.

'Look there. The water's already lapping into the caves. You were right. It does come round the rocks quickly. So lovely, though, isn't it?'

'Gorgeous. I'd forgotten how lovely. The beach looks so neat and tidy when the tide's in. Do you want to walk for a while or go back to the car?'

'I'd like to walk, if that's all right with you?'

She nodded and they strolled along the cliffs, looking down at the waves as they rolled endlessly in and out. He took her hand again and she smiled as she squeezed his. She felt a warm feeling rush through her. Was this love? Was this what it meant?

It was just after half past six when they parked outside a hotel, high on the cliffs above yet another perfect cove.

'It's a bit early for dinner, but I dare say we can while away some time with a drink,' Tristan remarked.

'This is a gorgeous spot. Have you been here before?' she asked.

He shook his head. 'I was checking for places to eat on the Lizard and saw this. It's a bit out of the way, so I thought it might not be too crowded. Look, can you see that rock out there? It looks a bit like a cat.'

'And the lighthouse is just over there.

I suppose I must have seen this place from over there, but never realised it was actually a hotel, despite the huge letters across the front. I've certainly been to the lighthouse before. The garden's pretty too. We could sit out here for a drink.'

They went inside to order. Dinner wasn't served until seven-thirty so they took their drinks outside, together with the menus.

'Nice menu,' Bryher said. 'I'm quite spoiled for choice.'

'We could each choose something different and share,' he suggested.

'How very intimate.'

'I hope we may become so.' He raised an eyebrow.

Bryher's heart was doing its best to escape, or so it seemed. She needed to try to remain in control of her feelings before she made some sort of idiot of herself. But he had definitely said he loved her — or thought he did. It made her feel uncertain. She thought about her friend, Bill, whom she had known for years. She knew that her feelings for him were deep affection, but in no way could it be called love. If looking at someone could make her heart race . . . if touching him even casually had a profound effect . . . was that it? Was that what people called love?

'Kiss me,' she said suddenly.

'What — here? Now?'

'Yes, please.'

'Well, all right. But why so suddenly?'

She leaned towards him and put her hand on his neck, drawing him close. He responded, and kissed her long and tenderly.

'Actually, I've been wanting to do that all day,' he murmured huskily. 'So, did I pass?'

'Oh yes,' she replied breathlessly. 'You passed all right.'

'Hmm. Excuse me.' The waitress stood beside them. 'I wondered if you're ready to order yet?'

Blushing madly, Bryher pulled away. Tristan also looked embarrassed and picked up the menu.

'Did you decide on the chicken?' he asked. She nodded. 'And I'll have the fish. Any starter?' She shook her head.

'No, thanks. Just the main course, please.'

'Thank you, sir, madam. Would you prefer to eat inside?' They agreed and picked up their drinks and went back into the hotel.

'Think it might be safer,' Tristan murmured with a significant look. 'After that kiss, I'm not sure it would be wise to be so close to you in public ever again. We should talk about something safe.'

'Like work? We can discuss plans for the Porthtroon building.'

'A really romantic dinner. Lovely hotel. Magnificent view. We just shared the most devastating kiss I've ever experienced and she wants to talk about work. What does a guy have to do?'

'Was it really?'

'Was what, what?'

'The most devastating kiss you've ever had?'

'Yes. Actually it was. I haven't quite come down to earth yet. Here comes our ever so slightly embarrassed waitress.'

The woman laid out their cutlery, smiled rather knowingly and left them.

'She's obviously seen it all before. She was looking to see if you have a ring on. So now she is quite certain we're having an affair. That you're the other woman.' His eyes twinkled.

'How do you know all this?'

'One of my friends at university did bar work. He said you could always tell when people were married because they looked around the room and listened to other people's conversations. They don't talk much to each other. If they were having an affair, they whispered and touched each other and sometimes even kissed.'

'And if they were just a courting couple?'

'They usually giggled a lot and were a bit uncertain of each other.'

'Perhaps I need to giggle a bit and

allay her suspicions.'

'Does that mean we might be a courting couple, then?'

'Maybe. Here comes the food. I shall giggle immediately.'

* * *

It was nine-thirty when they arrived back at Bryher's cottage. Tristan stopped outside and switched off the engine.

'You do realise my bike is still at your place?' she commented.

'I'd forgotten. You could collect it tomorrow. Suppose I come over for some surfing and then I can drive you back? Then we might go for a spin. There's an old airfield I know. We could speed without getting caught.'

She gave him a grin. 'Sounds perfect. Surf and speed. Tide will be best around ten, I think. D'you want to come in for coffee?'

'I thought you'd never ask.'

She felt strangely nervous as they walked up the path. Her feelings for

Tristan were all confused. She didn't want to push him away — but she wasn't ready for anything more just yet. For now, her invitation was coffee and nothing more. She needed time to think.

8

For the next few weeks, Bryher tried to maintain a mostly businesslike relationship with her boss. They spent working time together and met at weekends for surfing sessions and occasional bike rides. She insisted that meals out were put on hold for a while.

Tristan seemed to accept the new arrangements without complaint, but he made it clear that he was hoping always that their relationship could develop into something much more, when she was ready. He didn't want to risk spoiling anything by rushing her. He was surprised by her reticence. At first, she had given him several indications that she found him attractive.

At the start of the week, they were having their usual breakfast meeting.

'I'd like you go out on your own to

look at some properties,' Tristan announced. 'I think you're ready to make some assessments without me. You can always say your husband will look later if you're interested.'

'Ive made it clear that I don't like that idea. Honesty or nothing for me.'

'Oh, for goodness' sake. Don't be so naive. Everyone does it. Let the agent know you're into property development, and the price sticks high. There's also an auction coming up. Several places there may be worth consideration.'

'Haven't we got enough work to do with what we've got? The work has scarcely begun on the Porthtroon place.'

'Planning issues there. Some sort of preservation order, so the look of the property has to be partially preserved. Architect is struggling a bit.'

'It's hardly a place of beauty, is it?'

'Certainly not. But it's the character of the harbourside that is of concern. If we use the old timbers, as the idiots in planning suggest, it all has to be supported from the inside. The whole front is rotten. I sometimes wonder where their brains are.'

'Sounds like the whole place should be torched, as the old chap I met in the beginning had suggested.'

'You could be right. Now, this is a list of the places I'd like you to look over. You know what I'm needing. Potential to rebuild. Possibility of putting in more than one new property if there's sufficient land. Take the camera. Check with estate agents. They usually have open days when there's an auction coming up.'

'And check the space around for parking builders' vans and so on.'

'Good girl.'

'Tristan, I'd like to thank you for the chance to do more. I'm enjoying it all. Very much.'

'You're doing well. Now, on your bike, as they say.'

'I'm in the car today,' she said with a grin. 'When are you off to your other job, this week?'

'Tomorrow. And Thursday. Nigel's

coming to check progress on Wednesday so you need to be around then.'

After making a few appointments from the leads Tristan had given her, Bryher set out. It was a wet day. She was glad of the car instead of having to ride around in damp leathers. She'd arranged to meet one of the agents at a row of old cottages that were in the forthcoming auction. They were in poor condition and with five in the row, they were expected to make a good price for conversion into one or two big properties. The cottages smelled damp and musty and looked almost derelict.

'The walls can easily be knocked through,' the agent was saying.

'Do you mind if I take some pictures?' Bryher asked. 'Only I'm not sure if my, er . . . partner will think this is worth it.'

'Well, I suppose. We're not keen because of the security angle. What's wrong with our pictures in the brochure?'

'I was thinking more of the structural

side of it. You know, woodworm in the beams and all that. Get some more idea of what's involved.'

The young man in his smart suit and tie, reeking of aftershave, gave a slightly condescending smile and nodded.

'You thinking of this for a home for yourselves?' he asked.

'Maybe.' Oh dear, she thought. She was getting as bad as Tristan. Fibbing was coming to her more easily, and she hated herself for it.

She pulled herself together. 'Has there been much interest?'

'Masses. We've sent out dozens of brochures and there have been lots of viewings. Should be a lively auction.'

'Well, thanks very much.'

'If your partner wants to view, give me a call. There's a couple of weeks to go, unless we get a prior offer of course.'

'Do you know if the properties are listed buildings?' If they were, then there would be little point in redeveloping as the restrictions were a pain.

'No. They are old, but not especially significant.'

'Well, thanks for your time.'

'We hope to see you at the auction.'

As she drove away, she thought carefully about the property. She went into a cafe and ordered coffee and a sandwich. She took out her pad and made careful notes, the way Tristan had taught her. Potential conversion possibilities. Parking. Actual area, and what facilities there were. She would type it up when she got back to the office and print off her pictures. She looked at her watch. Time for a bit more scouting, as they called it. She had a missed call from Tristan that must have come through while she was out of range. So many places in Cornwall had mobile phone blackspots.

When she was on her way back on the road, the phone rang with a message. She stopped the car and listened, in case it was something she needed to do before her next visit.

'Bryher, can you meet me at

136

Porthtroon, please? Soon as. There's a fire at the building. Our building.'

She wasn't far away from the village, so turned round and drove back. A fire? That was awful. Or was it? What had Tristan said about it? The timbers were rotten and would need supporting. And hadn't she mentioned that very morning, that someone had suggested torching the place?

Her heart began to race. Surely Tristan would never do anything like that?

When she was near the village, she was stopped by the police.

'Sorry, miss, but there's a fire here and access is restricted.'

'Yes I know. I work for the people restoring the building. My boss has just asked me to come down.'

The policeman conferred with his colleague and they nodded.

'All right, miss, but you'll have to park at the top of the village and walk the last bit. There's not much room down there, and the fire trucks need as much space as possible to manoeuvre.'

'Thanks very much, officer. I promise I'll keep out of the way.'

Bryher parked as directed and walked down the narrow road. There was a huge pall of smoke rising from the harbourside and flames were still visible through the broken windows. Water was being pumped from the harbour and high-powered jets were playing over the front of the building. There were crowds of people gathering, watching.

'Nobody inside, thank heavens,' she heard someone saying. She scanned the faces, searching for Tristan. He was near to one of the trucks, talking with the fireman. She crossed over to him.

'Oh, good. You got my message.'

'Just a few minutes ago. I was in a blackspot for reception. Do they know how it started?' she asked.

'Not yet. Whatever it was, it took hold very quickly. The inside is practically destroyed and this front is in danger of collapsing altogether, evidently.' Tristan was looking most concerned. 'At least none of our chaps was there. In fact, as far as we know, nobody was anywhere near.'

There was a sudden gust of wind from the sea and despite the water being sprayed, flames rose again, making a terrifying cracking sound. The front caved in and the flames rose as they found new materials to burn.

'Wow,' Bryher exclaimed. 'That answers that one.' The whole building gaped open and they could see right inside. The entire structure was gone and the roof was finally collapsing. She looked at Tristan. A mixture of emotions crossed his face. She could see that included somewhere among them, there was a sense of relief. There was clearly nothing left for the planners to preserve. The terrible thought that it was no accident came into her mind again. Surely he would never deliberately set a fire?

'It's a mess,' he said. 'I don't know what the planning situation will be now. They might insist we recreate the look of the building but if we can do it with new materials, it will be so much easier. On the other hand, we may get free rein and do what we originally planned.'

Bryher could say nothing. A policeman approached.

'I understand you're the owner of this building?'

'That's right. Well, my company owns it.'

'We believe the fire was set deliberately. Can you comment, sir?'

'Can I comment? Whatever do you mean? You can't think I started this lot? I was in my office at the time.'

'And was anyone with you?'

'Well, no. But I did receive a phone call there to tell me about the fire. That must be on record.'

'I see. And the young lady? Is she anything to do with you?'

Tristan turned to her. 'Bryher Jenkins. She's my personal assistant.'

'And where were you at the time?'

'I've been looking at a property. I met the agent there. He can vouch for me.

After that, I called at a café for a sandwich. The phone call came to me when I was back on the main road. I came here right after that.'

The officer made notes on what each of them had said and asked for the name of the estate agent and the café.

'Thank you, sir, madam. That will do for now. We'll certainly want to talk to you again. Where can we get hold of you?'

They each gave him a mobile number and their home addresses.

Bryher found her knees were shaking and she felt positively light-headed.

'Are you all right?' Tristan asked. 'You look as white as a sheet.'

'I feel really strange.'

'Shock. Let's go and get a cup of tea or something.'

They went into one of the little cafes by the harbour and ordered tea and scones. Though Bryher protested that she couldn't eat a thing, Tristan insisted, and she actually quite enjoyed her scone when it arrived.

'What a day,' she said shakily. 'I can't believe we were questioned by the police.'

'It isn't over yet. They are sure to think the fire was deliberately set to get rid of the old place.'

'And was it?'

He stared at her in horror. 'You surely don't think I'm capable of something like that?'

'Well, no,' she said hesitantly. 'But it does actually help us quite a lot, doesn't it?'

'Maybe — but I wouldn't do that. You must surely believe me.'

She felt slightly sick. How well did she truly know Tristan? He certainly was able to fib like a pro when it came to buying property. Was he capable of lying about other things? Maybe. She didn't know him all that well when she thought about it.

'I believe you, if you say so. Of course I do.' She smiled weakly, hoping she sounded convincing. He was still staring at her intently. She didn't believe him, and he could tell.

'Bryher, I think we need to talk. Let's get back to the office and discuss this. I can't bear it if you think I'd lie to you.'

They walked back to their cars and drove in convoy back to Tristan's house and the office. Feeling awkward, disloyal and totally ill at ease, Bryher sat at her desk. He came and sat close to her.

'Come on, now. Honestly. What makes you think I could have done this? Burned down our property?'

'I don't. Not really. It's just that we were discussing it this morning and I mentioned that burning it down would solve many of our problems. I was really being flippant, though. It just seems like some terrible coincidence.'

'I'm disappointed that you could think that way. But I doubt there's anything I can say to alter your opinion. Let's move on. How did the visit to the cottages go? Any use?'

'I'm not sure. They're in a poor state. No preservation order, though.' She launched into her findings, adding that she would type out the report the next morning.

'Fine. I think we should call it a day for now. I'll see you tomorrow before I go off to be an accountant for the day. Oh, by the way, my sister, Carole, has invited us for lunch this Sunday. Can you face it?'

'Oh yes, the flower lady. Why should she invite me?'

'I told her about you and she'd like to meet you properly. Without a bike helmet, preferably.'

'Can I let you know? I'm not sure what I'm doing on Sunday. But thanks for the invitation.' Her brain was whirling in circles. Carole was his only relative and it seemed a bit like being invited to meet his family — possibly to gain their approval. She wanted desperately to avoid that while she was feeling such conflict inside. But she needed an excuse that wasn't simply surfing or meeting friends.

★　★　★

When she arrived home, the perfect excuse was waiting on her answering machine. She saw the light flashing and pressed the play button.

'Bryher, darling. It's Mum. I'm afraid Dad's had an accident and he's in hospital. I wondered if you'd be able to come and see us at the weekend. It's not too serious, but he's a bit down in the dumps. Speak later.'

Horrified, she quickly dialled.

'Mum? What's happened? Is Dad all right?'

'He's broken his leg. They're keeping him in hospital for more tests to make sure there's nothing else damaged. The car's a complete write-off.'

'Oh, dear. So how are you coping with getting to visit him?'

'Martin's driving me in each evening. We'll have to get another car eventually, of course, but it means waiting until the garage can get the one that we want.'

'Surely you can get a hire car?'

'I'm not driving some strange thing. I'll wait till we get another like ours.'

Bryher gave a sigh. Her mother was not a confident driver at the best of times but she needed something to get around. Once her father was out of hospital, he'd be like a bear with a sore head if he couldn't visit his beloved factory, and Martin would be fully occupied with managing the work. Maybe she needed to consider taking some time off and going to help them out for a week or two.

'I'll see if there's something I can do to help,' she promised. 'There's a bit of a problem at work so I can't come immediately. I'll certainly be there at the weekend. Give Dad my love and keep in touch.'

She put the phone down and decided she needed a glass of something. What a day. There was some wine open in the fridge, so she poured a glass and sat in her favourite window seat, thinking about the day. It was still only Monday and it seemed as if it had been a long week already.

The police had said that she and

Tristan needed to be available for more questioning, so she couldn't leave the area for at least a few days. Besides, there were things she needed to do at work — especially if she was going to ask for holiday. She'd only been there for a short while and presumably had not built up enough time to be owed any time off.

She dialled Tristan's mobile. 'Hi. It's me. I'm afraid my dad's had an accident and I'm needed at home at the weekend. So — I'm sorry but I have to refuse Carole's invitation.'

'Something serious?'

'Not sure. He's broken his leg but they're doing more investigations in case there's any more damage.'

'Go and see him if you need to. We'll manage without you somehow.'

'We've got the police to worry about. They said we should stay in the area for now.'

'Don't worry about that. I'm sure they'll understand.'

'I'll maybe go later in the week. I

have several things I need to tie up before I disappear. And there's Nigel's meeting on Wednesday. I need to be there for that — or so you said.'

'Type your notes for us tomorrow and we can deal with it. I think you should be with your family right now. Really, I mean it. Come in tomorrow, and then you can go to your parents' on Wednesday. We can phone the police and explain. I mean it. Organise yourself to go off after tomorrow.'

'Well, if you're sure. Thanks very much. My mum doesn't like driving so she is a bit stuck. I'll come in early tomorrow to make sure everything's in order. Thanks again. Goodnight.'

'Night, Bryher. Look, maybe you'd like to . . . No, maybe not. Bye.'

He had been about to ask her out, she felt certain. It was not a good idea, not while she was feeling so unsure about him. Besides, she needed to call her mother again and tell her she was able to visit sooner than expected.

She looked out at the beach. It was

flat calm, not a wave in sight; no chance of releasing her pent-up energy on a surf board. And she'd drunk wine, so no biking for her. Instead, she put on her battered trainers and went for a run. She jogged up the steep track to the top of the cliff and ran along the cliff path towards the next cove. She pushed herself and realised how out of condition she was feeling. It was ages since she'd been running, and she made a promise to herself that she would take a run each evening during the summer months. She stared down at the sea and her beach as if trying to saturate her mind with it before she went away.

* * *

'Oh, darling, that will be super,' her mother said when Bryher told her the news. 'Your boss must be a wonderful man to let you take time off. I look forward to hearing all about him. What time will you arrive?'

'Around midday on Wednesday. I

won't promise to come tomorrow as I'm not sure when I'll be finished.'

She worked hard all through the following day. Tristan was at St Ives, so she had the place to herself. She printed off her reports on the properties she had visited, took endless phone calls and made sure that Tristan would have everything necessary for the meeting the next day.

It was slightly odd that Tristan was so emphatic that she should go to her parents tomorrow, after being rather insistent that she would be needed for the meeting. *Perhaps it was something to do with that fire*, she thought, but tried to push the thought out of her mind.

She decided to wait in the office until he arrived back from his day at his other job. She made some coffee and a piece of comforting toast and was sitting at her desk, thinking through the events of the previous day, when the door opened and Tristan came into the office.

'Oh, I see. A late breakfast again,' he teased. 'So that's what you do when I'm away working.'

'Comfort food. I missed lunch, and this is all there was. Do you want some? There's that lovely honey I bought the other day.'

'Yeah, go for it. I'll have two slices, please. And a coffee.'

They sat companionably eating and drinking as she went through the various papers she had prepared.

'You're very efficient,' he told her. 'You've taken to this job like a duck to water. I think we're going to do very well. Make lots of money.'

'Maybe. But the property market is not at its best at present.'

'No — but there will always be a demand for homes in Cornwall.'

'At the expense of locals. Incomers buy everything in sight and local young folk can't afford anything.'

'I do have some ideas that might help in that area, but that's for the future. Now, why don't you get off home and pack? Let me know how your father is and when you're likely to be back.'

'Thanks, Tristan. You've been very kind. Good luck with Nigel tomorrow. Sure you don't want to change your mind and have me at the meeting?'

'Quite sure. There are things I need to discuss with Nigel.' His voice had an edge to it. Bryher wondered what was going on. Tristan certainly had something on his mind.

9

Bryher's mother was standing looking out of the window when she arrived. 'Oh darling, it's so good to see you. This is the famous new car, is it? It's rather bright, don't you think? But, never mind. I can't tell you how relieved we all are that you've got rid of that dreadful bike.' Mrs Jenkins had a great ability to speak without drawing a breath.

'Mum. Good to see you. I haven't got rid of the bike, by the way. This is a company car so there's nothing permanent about it. I'm keeping the bike in case I need it again. But never mind all that. How is Dad?'

'Much better. He's due home today, but I'm not sure we'll get him into your little car. Martin will have to do it. I'll call him.'

'I'll get my bag in,' Bryher said to the

153

now empty room. 'Oh Mum, you never change.' She had the feeling this would be a difficult few days.

Her brother Martin collected her father from hospital, delivered him home later that day and settled him in the living room.

'How's my little sister?' Martin asked warmly, hugging her.

'I'm fine, thanks. You're looking well. And the family?'

'Yes, we're all well too. So, what's with the snazzy little motor outside? Don't tell me my sister's growing up at last?'

'Company car, would you believe. Just a modest little runabout, so the clients don't think I'm too well off.'

'I can't wait to hear about all of this. Mum said something about you being a PA to an accountant. How does that work? You were never the accountant type.'

'Come on, you two. Stop chatting and help settle your father. I think we'll have to get a bed downstairs. I don't see him getting up our twisty staircase. What do you think?'

'I'll be fine, dear,' Bryher's dad protested. 'Just stop fussing for five minutes. What I need most in the world is a decent cup of tea and to see my children properly. Come on, Bryher, let's hear about this new job of yours.'

'Actually, Dad,' Martin began, 'I really should get back. I left Jacob in charge and we have a couple of orders to get out before tomorrow. I'll see you again, won't I, Sis? You're not rushing away, are you?'

'I'm not sure how long I'll be able to stay. Work and that. But we'll catch up soon. Maybe go out for a drink one evening?' They gave each other a hug. 'I miss you, you know. You should come down to Cornwall and see me sometime. Give my love to all the family.'

Mrs Jenkins came in with a tray of tea and some fresh, home-made cakes. 'Now where's he gone?' she asked.

'Needed to get back to work.' Her father looked quite worn out.

'Really? He's too bad. He might have waited for tea, now I've gone to the bother of making it.' She busied herself pouring tea and passing round the bone china cups. Bryher felt the years slip away as she remembered the formal ways of home. Her mother would never approve of the oversized mugs in her own kitchen. Saved getting second cups, she always thought.

She tried her best to relax, not to let her parents' ways affect her so much. She had not lived at home since she went to university.

Supper was a casual affair, eaten from trays in the living room, so that her father was not left alone. Her mother did not really approve, but gave in with good grace and was eager to ask more about her job and her boss.

'So, how old is he? Is he married? What does he look like?' Her mother's usual string of questions, asked without a pause.

'Probably about thirty-something, unmarried and quite good-looking.'

'So, what's wrong with him if he hasn't married and is good-looking?'

'Oh, Mum. You never change, do you? There's nothing wrong with him. He's been concentrating on his career and well, never got round to it.'

'And does he have a girlfriend?'

'Not that I know of,' she replied wearily.

At last the television was put on and they settled to watch one of her mother's favourite soaps. Bryher let her thoughts wander. How had Tristan's day gone? Had the meeting with Nigel gone well? What did he think of the various properties? And the fire? She wondered if she should phone him, but decided against it. She still felt somewhat confused.

Talking to her parents had put some things into perspective. She realised she really did find him attractive. Very much so. She had been holding back for so long because she needed to know where things might lead. Work and private life was a difficult mix, and she needed to prove herself at work first.

'So who do you think was the guilty one?' her mother was asking. 'Bryher, I'm speaking to you.'

'Sorry, Mum. I've no idea. I never watch this programme.'

'But you used to love it. What do you think, Harry?' she persisted. But her husband was fast asleep.

'I wonder if he should be in bed?' Bryher suggested. 'It's going to be an effort for him to get upstairs. You've got a television in your bedroom if he wants to watch for a while.'

'Oh dear. This is all so difficult. I don't know how we're going to manage.' Her mother wrung her hands.

'Well, I'm here for a few days, so we'll get a routine going and then you'll be fine. First days are always the worst.'

With some difficulty, they finally got her father settled into bed. Mrs Jenkins was herself exhausted, so they all decided to have an early night.

Bryher still felt edgy, concerned about the life she'd left behind in

Cornwall. It was more than simply being away from the sea. She realised she was missing Tristan. They had developed a closeness that was quite different from any other relationship she had ever known. She remembered the kiss they had shared — so long ago now — and knew she wanted more. Was absence making the heart grow fonder? Maybe. She picked up her mobile and dialled his number.

'Sorry, I can't take your call right now. I'll call back if you leave your name and number.'

She switched off. No point leaving a message. If he was out, he was out. She wondered where he might be and felt stupidly jealous. She had no idea what he did with his time off. Maybe he had given up on her and found himself a new lady friend. *Silly term*, she thought. *I wasn't his lady friend, or girlfriend or whatever it was supposed to be called. I've no right to feel jealous.*

She'd call tomorrow, just to check on the office and ensure all was well.

Her mother continued to pump her for information about her boss all the next day. As her father's health improved, he quickly became restless, as Bryher had predicted.

'You can't possibly go into work,' Mrs Jenkins insisted. 'Maybe next week if Martin can organise it.'

'I'll have gone completely mad by then. Bryher — you can help me out here. Once I'm in the office, I'm quite capable of organising everything. Tell your mother you agree, for pity's sake.'

'Wait until tomorrow. Then you only have one day before the weekend. I'm seeing Martin for a drink tonight, so I'll see what he thinks.'

Bryher's mobile rang. As she listened, she went pale.

'I see. Well, all right. I can come back tomorrow morning. I'm sure my parents will be able to manage without me by then. Thanks.'

'What is it? You look terrible. What's happened?'

'We have some trouble. I really need to go back tomorrow at the latest. You'll be all right, won't you?'

'I suppose so. But what is it?' her father asked.

Bryher felt surprisingly tearful. 'That was Tristan. My boss. He thinks he's probably going to be arrested.'

'I knew it! I knew there was something wrong with him. Knew if you got a decent job, something had to go wrong.'

'Stop it, dear,' her father ordered. 'You don't know any such thing. Perhaps you need to explain it to us, Bryher.'

'One of the properties we're developing caught fire the other day. It was in a very dilapidated condition. It was giving problems with planning and then it caught fire. They suspect he burned it deliberately.'

'And did he?'

'I really don't think so. He working at the office in St Ives, so he has an alibi. But they think he may have organised it all.'

'And you?' her mother asked. 'They don't suspect you, do they?'

'No. I was with an estate agent.'

'You must find another job right away. You can't be associated with any criminal types. I knew it was all too good to be true.'

'You said that already, Mum. I don't think for a minute that Tristan would do something like that,' she said vehemently, knowing that at last, she truly believed it. 'Actually, you know, I think I should go back today. You don't really need me here.'

'But you're seeing Martin this evening.'

'I'll call him. See if we can organise something to get Dad into his beloved office tomorrow.'

It was almost four o'clock by the time she was driving along the A30 back to her beloved home. She'd only been away for a couple of days but somehow, it felt longer. It was sad to think she'd grown so far apart from her parents.

Perhaps everyone did, in some way.

Reaching her flat, she immediately dialled Tristan's number, greatly relieved when he answered.

'I'm back, Tristan,' she said.

'Oh, Bryher, thank you. Can you come over to the office? I really need to talk to you.'

'Why don't you come here? I'll cook something and we can talk.'

'If you're sure. Thanks, that would be great. I'd take us out but I daren't let anyone overhear anything we say. What time?'

'Right away if you like. It won't be anything special. Omelette okay?'

'Perfect. See you soon.'

She looked in the fridge. Typical. No eggs. No cheese. There was bread in the freezer, but that was all. She'd probably just about have time to drive to the next village where there was a little shop.

She stuck a note on the door with 'back soon' scrawled on it. The shop was just closing but the owner knew her and allowed her to grab the things she needed. When she got back, Tristan was staring at her note.

'Sorry,' she told him. 'I forgot I'd run everything down before I left. I'd expected an indefinite stay, but a couple of days and I'd had enough.'

'That's a shame. I suppose we all grow away from those we love. I take it your father's all right?'

'Yes, I guess. Already fretting about work. My brother handles things very well, though, so they'll be fine. My mother is most difficult. But, enough of me. What's been happening here?'

'The police found traces of accelerant at the warehouse. They know all about the planning issues and so I'm number one in the frame.'

'But you were in St Ives at the time.'

'I know and they know. But I was supposed to have employed someone to do it. They can't arrest me as they don't have proof. Yet.'

'They think they can get proof?'

'Apparently. What a mess.'

'So, how did the meeting go with

Nigel? What was his take on it?'

'He cancelled. Sorry — after all your hard work to leave things ready.'

'What was his reason?'

'He decided to go on holiday. Apparently his wife had been nagging him for a break, so they took off. He has a place in Spain and they got a last minute flight.'

'Interesting. Look, do you want some wine? It isn't very cold, but I could always add some ice or something.'

She poured them a glass each, put the bottle in the fridge and began to prepare the simple meal. Tristan sat watching. He looked very weary, and Bryher felt her heart go out to him. He was clearly very worried.

'Do you think he could have organised the fire?'

'Nigel? No, he's a pillar of society. Church warden and everything.'

'So, who do you think did it? If it was really set on fire deliberately.'

'I just don't know. I wondered if it might have been kids. Someone playing around. But I guess that was wishful thinking. Can I do anything?'

'Grate some cheese, please. I got some lettuce and tomatoes. Hardly much of a salad but the best the shop could offer at this time of day.'

'It's all fine. First time you've cooked anything for me.'

'As I said, I'm no cook. Mostly I eat from the microwave. My mum was too good a cook to let me experiment. 'Go and do your homework,' was the usual cry. So I did. And plenty of reading in between.'

'Let's just enjoy an evening together and forget our troubles. You've been keeping me at bay for such a long time, I'd forgotten we were such good company for each other. Tell me about your father's business.'

It was a surprisingly pleasant evening, under the circumstances. They talked about inconsequential things and both learned a little more about each others' backgrounds. Bryher yawned.

'I'm sorry, but I suddenly feel

shattered. I'll come into the office tomorrow. We can decide what we're doing then.'

'Thanks again for this evening. And for coming back early. Hope your parents understood.'

Bryher watched him drive away. She hoped that their future lay together. All the same, she was glad she hadn't yet committed herself to anything.

★　★　★

The next morning, they had a rather half-hearted discussion about the Porthtroon property. It was still a crime scene as far as the police were concerned, so nothing could be done there. They both felt on edge, as if they were waiting for something to happen.

'Oh — I put in an offer on that old cottage we saw. Not for the business; for me to live in. I'll put it through the business to minimise expenses.'

'Wow, that's terrific.'

'You do like it, don't you?'

'I love it. It'd be a great place to work.'

'They haven't accepted my offer yet. It was a bit of a cheeky figure, but who knows?'

There were one or two other projects on the go and Bryher tried to concentrate on working on them. One was a house, almost completed and in need of marketing. She was putting together some details, ready to send to an estate agent, when there was a loud knock at the door.

'Mr Adams? Tristan Adams? I have a warrant for your arrest on suspicion of arson.' The officer went on to give the caution familiar to everyone who watched police shows on television.

'But how can you arrest me? There can be no evidence. I didn't do it.'

'Oh we have evidence all right. One large petrol can in your garage. An empty petrol can. Now, don't make this difficult, sir.'

Tristan sighed and wearily rose from his seat. 'You had no right to go poking around my garage. Okay, I'm coming.' He stopped. 'But don't most people have petrol cans in their garages?' He held up a hand in surrender. 'Okay. What's the procedure now?'

'Questioning down at the station. If we have enough grounds to charge you, then that's what will happen.'

'Ring Humphries, will you, Bryher? I need him to meet me at the station. I won't be answering any questions till my solicitor is present.' Tristan was white-faced by now, but seemed to be gathering some sort of control.

'Shall I come with you?'

'I'll call, or get someone to call, when we know what's happening. You keep things going here.'

'Okay. Don't worry. Mr Humphries will soon sort this mess, I'm sure.'

Before they had driven out, she was on the phone to the solicitor. He was suitably horrified and promised to drop everything and rush to the police station. She sat still, staring into space. A petrol can in Tristan's garage? How could he be so stupid as to leave potentially incriminating evidence in his own garage? Surely that was proof of his innocence? Whatever else he might be, Tristan was not stupid.

She decided to do some investigating of her own. There were a number of files she had never looked at, believing they were private and therefore, not within her work brief. Nigel's sudden departure had made her suspicious. It seemed an obvious escape route for him if he was the guilty one. But why would he stoop to such a thing? He was very well off and seemingly had enough money to finance any number of projects.

Unless something had gone wrong. There was this so-called credit crunch. Perhaps he'd lost money on some deal. But there would be nothing in the files to indicate that. Unless Tristan was also his personal accountant?

Hating herself for being so nosy, she began her search. What would she do if she did unearth any incriminating evidence? She would lose Tristan forever if she betrayed his trust. On the other hand, dared she get in any deeper if there was something unpleasant going on?

She found nothing of any help. Despite being incredibly nosy, she didn't feel she achieved anything. *Stupid woman*, she chided herself. *What was I expecting to find?* She hoped nothing had been disturbed, as she would hate Tristan to know she had been snooping.

The phone rang. 'Hi, it's me.' Tristan's voice had lost its usual confident tone. 'They're keeping me here a while longer. Do you think you could make sure everything's locked away safely? I think I left my keys on the desk, and the house isn't locked. I may be home later but I've been told I need to be prepared for at least an overnight stay.'

'That's terrible. Is there anything I can do? Bring anything for you?'

'Don't think so. Thanks, love. Don't

worry. We'll get through this.'

'Okay. I'll make sure everything is safe. We'll talk when you get back.'

She put the phone down and whispered 'my love', as if finishing the message. She put everything back into the filing cabinets and locked the drawers. She switched off the computers and wondered if she would ever work here again. No doubt there would be plenty of ends that needed tying but somehow, it all felt rather final.

She went over and locked the house, deciding she should take the keys with her. If he did come home, he may not have spare keys hidden anywhere and it would be silly to be locked out. Besides, it ensured she would see him as soon as he was released.

Feeling unsettled, Bryher drove home. If the worst happened, she'd have to get used to life without a car once more and possibly, looking for jobs.

She had scarcely stopped outside her house when Bill arrived, clad in wet suit and with his board under his arm.

'Hi stranger. You coming out?' he said breezily.

'Oh — hi. I don't think so. I need to be near the phone.'

'Trouble? Not the boss sort of trouble?'

'Yes, the boss sort of trouble. I can't really say much about it.'

'Then don't brood, and get yourself out in these magnificent waves. Nothing like it for washing away the troubles of the day.'

'Could be a bit more trouble than that. But okay, you're on. I'll dump my briefcase and change. Don't wait for me. I'll be down, as soon as.'

'No way will I leave you. Not when you're clearly upset. If he rings, you can just make him wait. I'm not having you waiting in case he deigns to call.'

'Dear Bill. You're my best friend. It's nothing like that. It's a different sort of trouble, I'm afraid. I may be out of a job at any minute. Let's not talk about it — I can't talk about it. I'll grab my stuff and we'll catch some waves.'

Bill watched her as she went up the stairs. She was in a different league to him, but all the same, he was very fond of her and couldn't bear to think that she could be unhappy in any way.

Out in the sea with Bill and one or two of her old friends, Bryher could forget about her troubles for a little while. After a couple of hours, they all went back to her cottage. Bill drove off to the nearest fish and chip shop and bought food for all of them. Someone else produced some cans of beer and they sat round, companionably chatting.

When the phone rang, silence fell in the room. They were aware that Bryher had some problem.

She took a deep breath, tried to hide the fact that she was shaking, forced a smile and excused herself. She took the phone into the kitchen.

'Hallo, dear. Just wondering how things are going?'

It was her mother. What on earth could she say? *My boss is in police custody? He's been arrested for arson?*

'I'm fine, thanks, Mum. It's gradually getting sorted. Look, can I call you back later? Bill and some of the lads are here. We're just having fish and chips. How's Dad?'

'He's driving me potty. Wants to get out all the time. Martin's been very good but the poor lad looks exhausted.'

'Okay, Mum. Give Dad my love. Speak later.' She hung up and went back into the living room. 'Sorry about that. My mum. Wanting to know if I'm all right.'

'And are you?' Bill asked. 'All right?'

'I don't know. Only time will tell.'

10

Bryher had little sleep that night. Saturday dawned bright and clear. She rose before six and decided a bike ride was what she needed to start the day. Hopefully, it would blow away the cobwebs.

It was still early enough for the roads to be clear so she set off at speed along the bypass, edging close enough to the speed limit for her to enjoy the sense of the bike's power. No way would she risk going over the limit, especially with all the other troubles she was experiencing. She glanced over to the other carriageway, almost expecting to see the red bike and helmet of the man she had decided she must truly love. If she didn't love him, why was she so upset about everything?

She rode back home more sedately and after a shower and breakfast, tried to plan for the weekend. It was difficult, not knowing what lay in store for Tristan. Surely he wouldn't be kept in custody much longer? She knew little about such things, but if he wasn't released it must mean they thought he was guilty. She truly didn't want to believe it but she must face reality.

It was ten o'clock before the phone rang.

'It's me, Bryher. They're finally letting me out. Can you come and collect me? I'm at Camborne.'

'I'll come right away. I take it they haven't charged you?'

'Actually, they have, but I'm not to be remanded in custody. There has to be a trial before that happens and I can hope and pray that the real culprit is found before then.' Tristan sounded exhausted.

'See you soon,' Bryher told him. She picked up his keys as well as her own and set off, not even sure where she was going — surely, it couldn't be so difficult to find the police station?

Her mind was churning over the events of the past week. It seemed ages since the fire and her visit to her parents. This could be the end of everything. Tristan could hardly run a business like this one if he had a criminal record. Nor should she, in any way, be involved with him.

What a mess. Love him or no, she had to cool things — at least until matters were cleared up.

★ ★ ★

'Hi. Thanks for coming to fetch me. They did offer a police car but I thought it might be easier this way, as long as you were willing.'

Bryher could hardly speak. The change in Tristan was staggering. He was unshaven and his two-day-old clothes were crumpled. His tie was hanging from a pocket, and he looked altogether gaunt and uncared-for.

'I've brought your keys, so we can go straight to your place. You'll feel better when you've had a shower and changed your clothes.'

'Thanks. It's been quite a day and night.'

He said little as they drove home. Bryher, still shocked, couldn't make any effort at conversation. Stopping in the drive, she handed him the keys.

'Won't you come in? Have a coffee, at least?'

'Well, I ought to get back,' she said automatically, wondering exactly why she needed to get back to her empty cottage on a Saturday morning. He looked so downcast, she smiled and changed her mind.

'Okay, I'll stay for a coffee.' He really needed company, she realised. 'I'll put some on while you go up and shower and change. Have you had anything to eat?'

'Not really. I think I was given toast but I can't remember eating it.'

He went upstairs and she heard water running. She looked in the fridge and found eggs. She beat some in a bowl and put bread ready in the toaster. Scrambled eggs had to make him feel better. The ultimate comfort food. After that, she should leave him and try to think through her own plans. Even if it was heartbreaking, she ought not to be around Tristan Adams until this mess was sorted out.

'That's better,' he said, coming down wearing clean jeans and a T-shirt. His eyes looked clearer and less sunken, though the black lines beneath them were still evident.

'I'm doing scrambled eggs for you. And the coffee's ready.'

'You're a star. Thank you so much.' He came behind her and put his arms round her waist. It made her vow to be distant, even harder.

'Hey, careful. I don't want to ruin my culinary efforts.'

He dropped his arms and she felt him withdraw. Feeling totally dreadful she continued cooking. 'Can you get a plate out? And cutlery. I didn't want to go nosing through the cupboards.' She blushed slightly, remembering nosing through the files the previous day.

'This is very kind of you. I wouldn't have blamed you if you wanted nothing more to do with me.'

She blushed again and wondered how to say what was on her mind. It seemed like kicking someone when they were down.

'Well, maybe we should cool things for a while. Until we know what's going to happen.'

His face took on an expression close to despair. 'Yes, we should. I don't want to drag you down too. It's been a horrendous experience. Being in a police cell was bad enough but the thought of prison . . . ' He was silent.

'Come on,' she encouraged. 'It might not come to that. Now, eat my wonderful creation or I shall be deeply hurt.'

He looked uncertain and picked up a fork, gingerly prodding at the food.

'Aren't you having some? It smells wonderful.'

'Enjoy. I'll pour the coffee.' How could she possibly leave him alone like this? He was totally traumatised and clearly needed company and care.

'I was thinking that maybe I should look for another job,' she forced herself to tell him. 'Just something temporary to tide me over.'

'Of course. I can't expect you to stay on. But keep the car for a while. You might need it.'

'Thanks, that's very generous of you.' She sipped the hot coffee and watched as he cleared his plate.

'Bryher, you do believe me, don't you? That I didn't set this fire?'

'Yes,' she said hesitantly, wishing she meant it. If only she hadn't mentioned that morning that a fire would solve everything.

'You don't believe me. I can see it. Okay, then I must tell you something. I don't want you to repeat it to anyone yet. I know who set the fire — or organised someone to do it on his behalf.'

'It was Nigel, wasn't it?'

'You guessed. He's in mega financial trouble.'

'Ah! I knew it.'

'I got it out of him. He needs a large sum of money urgently. He's made some rash investments abroad and with the state of the currency markets, he's lost a great deal. He's trying to keep it from his wife. He thought that if we cleared this property quickly, he might salvage something — sell the land on for a fortune to another speculator. You and I would never get anything much out of it for ourselves, but if Nigel had cleared a decent profit from a prime bit of land, he'd be safe for the time being.'

'But how could he allow you to take the blame? Who actually did it?'

'He'd never have believed they would blame me. I expect he paid some dodgy bloke to set the fire, and then clear away from the area. He assumed the police would think it was kids or someone squatting in the building.'

'I still don't understand why you

haven't told the police. Has Nigel got some hold over you?'

'Not really. He has done a few deals that may not be entirely straight. Because I was his associate, I might have been forced to take some of the blame. It was a long time ago, but he's been generous to me since then and I felt I owed him.'

'Not that much, surely. Not to be arrested and everything.'

'He has a wife who enjoys too many of the good things in life and with the failed overseas investments, he is in deep trouble. Once we've sold the properties we have on our books, I'm having no more to do with him. I should still have some capital of my own to work with, if the legal fees don't swallow it all.' He leaned forward, took her hands and his tortured eyes gazed into hers. 'Bryher, please don't leave me. I'd hoped we were going to have a future together in every way. Not just a business relationship. Now you know the real truth, doesn't it make a difference?'

She tried to speak calmly over the sound of her pounding heart. 'I need to think about it. I'm still shocked that someone like Nigel could do this. That he could leave you to pick up the pieces and clear out of the country. You've always treated him as if he was such a special person, yet you knew about all of this? When exactly did you find out?'

'He called me from the airport, telling me to put the site on the market and tackle all the biggest companies around to get the best possible price. We have plenty of contacts. He was quite right. A prime site like that could make a fortune. I really only twigged that he must have been behind the fire when the police were questioning me. Put two and two together. I assumed it must have been kids or something. I suppose I'm just too trusting.' He laughed bitterly.

Bryher stroked his hands comfortingly. 'So what do we do now?'

He smiled. 'I like the sound of 'we'. But the truth is, I simply don't know.

We have to get rid of everything we possibly can that is a shared deal with him. There are a couple of places almost ready to go. Once they're sold, Nigel gets his half of the profit and the rest belongs to me. Well, to my half of the company, anyway. I shall dissolve the partnership as soon as possible. If I can clear myself, I can remain as an accountant with Wyatt and Company in St Ives part-time and hopefully, you and I can start again. We have the office and basic equipment, contacts and expertise.'

Bryher sat quietly, contemplating his rosy picture of the future. So much depended on his name being cleared. He stared anxiously at her, trying to work out what she was thinking.

'How do you clear your name?' she asked.

'I suppose there is only one way. Proving it will be difficult. Nigel will have the best lawyers available. I suppose I'd better call him right away. Perhaps he still has a bit of decency somewhere.'

'Do it. At least then you'll be off the

hook. I'm going back to my cottage now. I'll wait for you to call.'

She dropped a kiss on his head and left him, wondering how this was all going to turn out. Tristan had confessed that he may have been guilty of something fairly minor in the past, but she felt certain that he was now telling the whole truth. As long as Nigel would also tell the truth, they might have a future.

But would Nigel agree to put himself in jeopardy? Back at her flat, she got out the vacuum cleaner and pushed it round vigorously as if she could somehow clear up everything that was troubling her.

Two hours later, there was a knock at the door. Tristan came in, looking much more cheerful.

'Nigel is horrified that I have been accused. He is flying home as soon as he can get a flight and I am confident that he will sort it out. I really think everything will be all right, Bryher. It seems he's not all bad after all.'

* * *

A week later Tristan phoned, early on Saturday morning.

'I'm officially cleared of all suspicion. Somehow, Nigel's persuaded the authorities that one of his own staff was responsible for the fire. Someone he had sacked who held a grudge. Needless to say, the culprit has left the area and disappeared somewhere up-country.'

'And they actually believed all that?' Bryher asked.

'Nigel can be very convincing. And he's always generous to good causes, despite being broke. He'll bounce back — without me, I hasten to add. Our business dealings together are over. Are you up for some surfing?'

'Really? I may have been thinking about it. Come on over.'

'Oh, and remember that cottage? We got it. My offer was accepted.'

Bryher let out a big sigh. The future was back on track. Her future. *Their* future, maybe?

She was waiting at the door when his car pulled up.

'Come here,' he ordered as he reached the door. He pulled her into his arms and gave her the second most devastating kiss he had ever experienced.

'But, it . . . ' She stopped speaking as his mouth covered hers again. When, breathless and glowing, he finally stopped kissing her, he reached into his pocket and produced a small box.

'I've been carrying this around for rather a long time. When you feel you can, please open it and give me your answer.'

She took it and opened it. The diamond sparkled back at her.

She reached up to draw his lips down to hers once more. 'I've already got the answer. I really do think I know, now, what love is.'

THE END

We do hope that you have enjoyed reading this large print book.

Did you know that all of our titles are available for purchase?

We publish a wide range of high quality large print books including:
Romances, Mysteries, Classics
General Fiction
Non Fiction and Westerns

Special interest titles available in large print are:
The Little Oxford Dictionary
Music Book, Song Book
Hymn Book, Service Book

Also available from us courtesy of Oxford University Press:
Young Readers' Dictionary
(large print edition)
Young Readers' Thesaurus
(large print edition)

For further information or a free brochure, please contact us at:
Ulverscroft Large Print Books Ltd.,
The Green, Bradgate Road, Anstey,
Leicester, LE7 7FU, England.
Tel: (00 44) **0116 236 4325**
Fax: (00 44) **0116 234 0205**

NO MISTAKING LOVE

Moyra Tarling

Working at Moonbeam Lake, it wasn't easy for single mother Laura Matthews. She wanted her twins to enjoy summer in the place she'd once loved — despite its painful memories. But she hadn't counted on Tanner Mcleod's reappearance. Six years ago, she'd comforted him when his brother died, and it had led to passion. But Tanner had left before she'd discovered the consequences of their love. How could she confess that *he* was the father the twins had never met?

KNAVE OF DIAMONDS

Wendy Kremer

Sharon is employed by a retailer to write some PR text about Patrick, a famous jewellery designer, who's creating an exclusive collection for the everyday woman. Patrick's initial resentment of Sharon changes when he gets to know her, whilst she admits that he's a fascinating man. If only other women didn't think so too! Then as Sharon and Patrick visit Hong Kong for a photo session things begin to buzz — only to fall apart. What has fate designed for them?